CW01102781

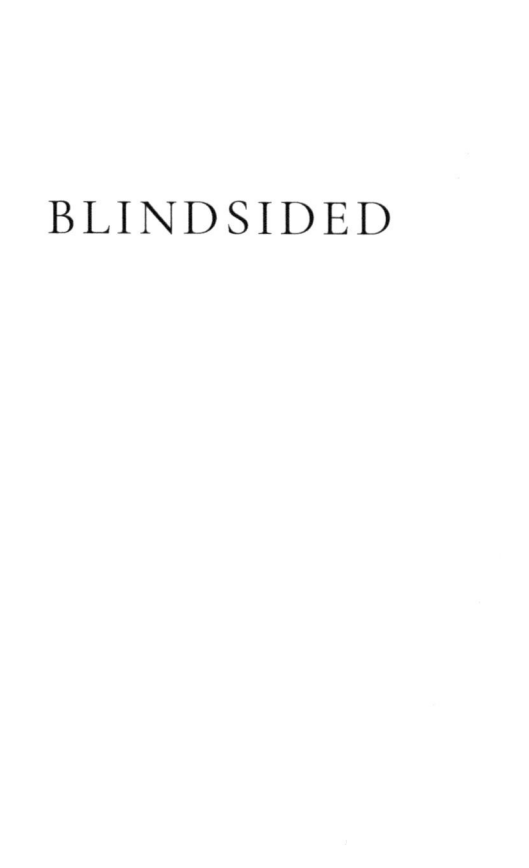

BLINDSIDED

BLINDSIDED

A Sean Colbeth Mystery

CHRISTOPHER H. JANSMANN

Copyright

Copyright © 2020 Christopher H. Jansmann All rights reserved

The characters and events portrayed in this book are fictitious. Any similarity to real persons, living or dead, is coincidental and not intended by the author.

No part of this book may be reproduced, or stored in a retrieval system, or transmitted in any form or by any means, electronic, mechanical, photocopying, recording, or otherwise, without express written permission of the publisher.

ISBN: 978-0-578-79309-2 (Kindle Edition)
ISBN: 979-8-552-99573-8 (Paperback)
ISBN: 978-1-0879-3820-2 (Hardcover)

Library of Congress Control Number: 2020921491

Printed in the United States of America

Dedication

For Paula:
Quiet, gentle support that pulled me through to the end. I truly could not have done this without you.

For Mom:
Published... a decade later than I thought. Thanks for waiting.

Contents

Copyright	v
Dedication	vii
One	1
Two	6
Three	12
Four	15
Five	21
Six	26
Seven	32
Eight	39

Nine	42
Ten	46
Eleven	52
Twelve	55
Thirteen	61
Fourteen	66
Fifteen	71
Sixteen	77
Seventeen	85
Eighteen	92
Nineteen	99
Twenty	107
Twenty-One	113

Twenty-Two	116
Twenty-Three	120
Twenty-Four	127
Twenty-Five	130
Twenty-Six	134
Twenty-Seven	143
Twenty-Eight	146
Twenty-Nine	153
Thirty	156
Thirty-One	162
Thirty-Two	165
Thirty-Three	172
Thirty-Four	176

Thirty-Five 180

Thirty-Six 186

Thirty-Seven
Epilogue 191

Acknowledgement 193
About the Author 195

One

Ingmar Pelletier - or, what was left of him, at least - was in the back of his late model Ford pickup truck beneath the carport of his Mid-Century Modern bungalow. His bare legs hung over the open tailgate, the pale white skin between the bottom of his shorts and the top of his crew socks having taken on the waxy complexion evident in most cadavers. Ingmar, even as eccentric as he was, had not been known to spend the evening out in such a manner and had therefore attracted the attention of his neighbor as she'd been out jogging at sunrise. Her subsequent call to 9-1-1 had led to my standing over the bed of the truck.

The underside of his white t-shirt had soaked up the blood that had pooled beneath his torso, giving it an oddly tie-died look; the front of his shirt appeared to have some sort of food stains on it, but not anything I recognized. His arms, frozen in rigor, were up around his head, almost as if he'd been bench pressing; this visual was enhanced by the way his torso had been snugged in between multiple five-gallon water jugs, some empty, some full.

I leaned in again, not really because I wanted to, and frowned once more. It's funny what first impressions you get at a crime scene; when I'd initially arrived, his half-open mouth had accentuated what I thought was a missing bridge or partial denture, making me wonder what would have brought him out of the cozy confines of his cottage without having them in. Hovering closer, though, I realized that the bullet from whatever gun he'd used had essentially performed a near-perfect dental extraction. I was reasonably certain that when the coroner arrived from Augusta, we'd find that a significant portion of the back of his head would be missing, seeing as though most of it appeared to be splattered against the rear of the truck's bed in a grisly patriotic red-and-white mess.

One shot, and likely nearly instantaneous.

I pulled back and circled the truck one more time. He had to have been sitting up at the time he pulled the trigger, and given his height, the bullet had shattered the rear window and windshield of the truck. The blood and dura matter splattered on the rear window gave me a general sense of orientation, but I'd not located the bullet hole or the bullet itself in the wall of the house adjoining the carport. The crime scene tech coming down from Bangor was going to have her hands full when she arrived.

It troubled me that it wasn't visible, though.

The Ford was something of an institution in Windeport; Ingmar was instantly recognizable in the faded blue homage to a different time – one that he was firmly part of. A tenured professor of agriculture at the University on the outskirts of town, he'd checked in as an undergrad sixty years earlier and never left. When I'd had him as an undergrad myself, he'd added running the Extension Service to his portfolio, managing all that entailed while continuing his teaching duties and research; I'd thought he was old *then* and had been amazed at his stamina. Looking at what was left of the professor I'd known reminded me that age is relative.

I flicked my eyes to my number two. "Where's the gun, Vasily?" I asked.

"I've not found it yet, Chief," he replied with a frown. Like me, he was dressed in a sweatshirt bearing the logo for our U. S. Masters Swimming club and matching nylon wind pants that had been hurriedly pulled over our swimsuits. His blond surfer-length hair was still damp and tied up in a haphazard bun, with stray locks whipping about in the gentle breeze coming off the ocean less than a quarter mile from where we stood. He inclined his head toward the two deputies who'd unceremoniously pulled us out of the pool when the call had come in; they appeared to be comparing notes from the neighborhood canvas they'd completed. "I can have them search again. But it seems to have walked off."

I felt my own frown deepen. "Guns don't do that," I sighed.

"Not suicide, then," Vasily said.

"I'm not ruling *anything* out until I see the coroner's report." I turned back to Ingmar. "But I find it highly unlikely he shot himself, then took the time to hide his gun from us before expiring."

Vasily chuckled. "I wouldn't put it past him," he said as he joined me at the bed and nodded sadly. "He was a strange duck, wasn't he?"

"Did you have him for BIO-100?" I asked. Vasily had been three years behind me.

"Yeah," he said. "I couldn't believe he sold us prior year exams."

I nodded. "Five bucks and the guarantee that questions for the current year would be drawn from any of the past year's versions. I think I learned more in that class than any other."

"Yeah." His eyes flicked back to mine. "What's your read?"

I stepped back again. "Something brought him out here, Vasily," I started as I headed for the door to the house. Pulling on a glove, I pushed the door open to re-enter the kitchen that was just off the carport. "Those beans look like last night's dinner," I said, pausing by the small Formica-topped table in the spotless kitchen that was straight out of the fifties. "Half eaten bowl replete with red hot dogs, buttered roll--" I ticked off the items that were sitting at the single place setting. "Bottle of Sam Adams--"

"Dinner of champions," Vasily observed.

"It *was* Sunday night," I pointed out. "And the Patriots were the late game."

Vasily pointed to the living room on the other side of the half-moon arch that separated it from the kitchen. "The television was still on and tuned to the station that carried the game last night. You can kind of see it from the kitchen." He leaned sideways around the arch. "Kind of."

I smiled. "Only the young eat in front of the television, Detective Korsokovach."

"Or an iPhone."

Scanning the kitchen and living room again, I added: "No signs of a struggle, and nothing seems out of place. If he was lured out to the carport, it was by someone he knew."

"And trusted?" Vasily pointed out.

"Maybe. Either way, I'll want the crime scene tech to go over the entire bungalow," I said and watched as Vasily made a note. "Heather won't be happy but remind her we'll treat her with lobster down at Aunt Millie's when she's done."

"That would motivate *me*," Vasily said. "Full workup?"

"Yeah," I replied, my eyes moving to the wall of windows from the living room that looked out onto Windeport Harbor. Ingmar wasn't directly on the beach, such as it was in Maine, but was separated from the rocky inlet by a dune heavily topped with slender leaves of grass that were bent against the constant breeze. Swells rose and fell in the harbor proper, seemingly oblivious to the tragedy that had unfolded in the cottage. Nature was strange that way, I suppose.

"Is Sylvia still here?" I asked as we moved back toward the carport.

"Yes," Vasily replied. "She's taking it well."

"All right. I'll talk to her next."

Vasily looked over my shoulder. "The coroner just pulled up," he said. "I'll pass along our request for a full Post."

I nodded and made my way over to the large oak tree in the front yard of the bungalow. A small bench was just below the massive crown; at this point in October, most of the leaves had fallen, but one tiny pocket of brilliant orange flamed just over the bench. As I neared a woman sitting there, I spied the annual bed that ringed the base of the tree. Ingmar's late wife had been quite the gardener, but after her passing, he'd clearly let the flowerbeds go. The irony wasn't lost on me given his stature within the agricultural community.

The woman looked up at me, and I smiled. Sylvia Gauthier had been my date to the Senior Prom more years ago than I cared to remember;

she'd left Windeport after high school but had returned recently to take the General Manager position at the Colonial Hotel and Resort. "Hey," I said as she made room for me on the bench and I sat down beside her. "How are you holding up?"

She fussed a moment with her long brown hair, tying it into a ponytail before flicking a speck of nothing off her black spandex running tights. "Okay," she said. "I admit, finding him has shaken me a bit. I think I'm still assuming I'm in some sort of movie. Or book."

"It will hit you later," I said. "Do you have anyone staying with you? Or someone you can stay with for a day or two?"

She laughed nervously. "You're making me feel like I'm going to have PTSD or something."

"You might," I said seriously.

Sylvia fussed with her zipper of her ultralight pullover, another sign that she wasn't actually handling finding a body all that well. Who would? "I'm alone at the moment, but I could crash at the hotel for a day or two."

"Having people around you is good," I said. "But I'd feel better if you had family."

Her green eyes connected with mine. "Yeah, everyone's in Florida already."

My eyebrows went up. "This early?" I asked.

"It's almost Halloween, Sean," she smiled.

"Damn," I smiled. "That explains why I can park in front of the IGA so easily these days."

"Snowbirds have flown," she nodded. "I won't see my parents until Memorial Day." She paused, smiling despite the situation. "If I'm lucky."

"Indeed." I stood and helped her up. "Vasily has your statement. If you think of anything else, though, call me."

"Thanks," she said, placing a hand on my bicep. "I will."

"I'll be in touch."

Two

I left Vasily behind and headed back to what we euphemistically referred to as the "public safety" building that housed the entirety of our police, fire, and municipal services for our small village. Windeport was just one of the hundreds of former fishing villages along coastal Route One, and as I drove the short distance from the cottage to the excellent example of nineteen-seventies Brutalist architecture that loomed along the main drag, I could still pick out signs of our town's original roots.

There were still commercial fishing concerns, but those dwindled more each year as the elders of the family retired and found their children had no interest in the rough life on the water. The modest dwellings sported rows and rows of lobster traps, set aside for the winter. I passed a deserted warehouse that had once been a thriving seafood exchange, and then drove past the multi-story vaguely Victorian homes where the wealthy scions from Boston would summer back in the day.

I turned left onto Route One, which wasn't much of a problem in October, and then turned right into the crumbling asphalt of the Public Safety building. The massive garage off to the edge of the pebbled-concrete structure was open, meaning either there was a four alarm somewhere in town or Fire Chief Rosenstein was down to the Dunkin Donuts with the entire day shift. Again.

Sighing, I pulled my town SUV into the designated Chief of Police spot and put it into park. In the ten years since taking over for my retiring predecessor, we'd had our share of small-town crime to investigate. Any village of our size would; you can't put close to three thousand people together and not have a few bad apples in the bushel. Add to that the influx of summer visitors, and the department generally had its hands full nearly year-round with one of the smallest staffs in the state.

Even as a native of Windeport, though, I couldn't remember the last *major* crime that had taken place in the village. Certainly not the last murder. I suspected if I did a quick search through our digital archives, I'd come up with something from the halcyon days of the nineteenth century. And if I couldn't find it in our system, I knew someone over at the library that would put her hands on it faster than I could ask the question.

I frowned, for that reminded me of the promise I'd made and the costume that was sitting in the Amazon-branded box on the passenger seat. Sighing once more, I locked up the SUV and went through the main entrance to the station proper.

Caitlyn Romero looked up from the semi-circular desk that dominated the small lobby and acted as intake for our non-emergency calls. "I thought it was your day off?" I asked as I headed past her and the doors beyond that led to our inner sanctum.

"I caught the call on the scanner," she said sheepishly. "I figured you could use a hand." Caitlyn pointed to the switchboard with the pen she'd been using on the crossword in the Bangor Daily. "I've already had two media inquiries and one confession."

Arching an eyebrow, I asked, "I trust you got the address so we could arrest them?"

"That could be hard," she replied. "Caller claimed it was an alien masquerading as their mother-in-law from Salem."

I rolled my eyes. "Call Gertrude back and tell her Bethesda is off her meds again; I hate to do it, but we should probably call Social Services now. That's the fifth call this month."

"I agree," she said as she put her headset on and started to dial. "What's our official response for media?"

"No comment," I laughed.

"I figured." I palmed my RFID on the reader and the door clicked open; the short hallway was empty save for the set of hard plastic chairs we reserved for visitors. The wall opposite had photos of all my predecessors, excepting the handful that had been in charge before photography had come into vogue.

The hallway emptied into the standard bullpen all police stations had. Since everyone was out at the bungalow, I had the space to myself and crossed to the kitchenette against the far wall. I'd fought the members of the Village Council in the last budget cycle to include monies for modernizing the station; my very first purchase had been the fancy Keurig to replace the Mister Coffee that had been there since the seventies. Popping a k-cup into the machine, I located a clean mug and a few moments later was happily paired with my first cup of the day.

My actual office was in the far corner, with windows looking out toward the high school. The only modern affectation was the laptop on the desk; the rest of the furniture was original to the building and reflected the late sixties motif that had been all the rage. The desk itself could have steamed across the Pacific as a battleship in the second world war. I wasn't sure but harbored a suspicion that the Formica flooring was the first ever designed by humankind.

I stared out at the athletic fields in the mid-morning light and saw the Field Hockey team was getting ready for their semi-final match. The coach had a nearly twenty year run of state championships on the line, and from what I could tell, that record wasn't in jeopardy. I sipped my coffee and considered the sport, wondering why the sticks were so short and realizing I'd been intentionally avoiding why I was at the office on my day off.

My iPhone buzzed in my pocket and I quickly retrieved it. "Vasily?"

"Heather has arrived. She expects to be here most of the day and wants to know if we can put her up for the night."

I frowned. Normally, we'd have rooms to spare any time after Labor Day, but with the International Potato Symposium in town, nearly every room in the surrounding county was booked. "I'll make some calls. Worst case, we can put her on the couch."

Vasily chuckled. "Wouldn't be the first time," he allowed. The two of us shared the massive apartment over the space that had once housed the full service pharmacy generations of Colbeths had run; when my father retired, he'd sold the book of business to an out-of-state chain that had built a modern abomination at the edge of town and left for Florida. We still owned the turn-of-the-last-century brick building, but nearly two years after he'd left, had no tenant in the retail space. "I'll let her know."

"Any luck on the gun?"

"Mark and Lydia took another careful look through the bungalow before Heather arrived and came up empty," he replied, referring to our two patrol officers. Both were fresh from the Justice Academy and had been rather starry eyed when called to the murder. "I'm having them do a circular search around the exterior now. One of them also suggested we might need to search the beach and dredge the cove."

"It's reasonable," I said. "If we assume someone tossed it, the beach is as likely a place as any. Contact the Harbormaster and see if one of the divers is on call."

"Will do."

I heard Vasily pause. "Yes...?" I prompted.

"Uh, Chief," he said carefully, "you, uh, wouldn't mind coming back for me? And, uh, all of my gear is back at the pool..."

I swore, having completely forgotten Vasily had come with me from the pool. "Yeah, give me thirty? I still need to contact Augusta and fill them in."

"I'm not envying that call," he replied as he disconnected.

I chuckled ruefully. While I was ostensibly an independent agency, Windeport was small enough that we were forced to rely on the State Police for the more exotic resources only their budget could support -- services such as ballistic analysis and state-of-the-art crime lab work. At our regular gatherings for Chiefs of Police, my colleagues in other jurisdictions had often regaled me with horror stories where this had been used as a cudgel to compel the transfer of cases deemed too complicated to handle locally to the State. I'd personally never had a situation crop up where there might be this sort of posturing, though frankly, I'd be quite happy to hand this particular case over to them, given how well I knew Ingmar. I highly doubted I would get my wish.

I put a call through to the cell of one Captain James Roberts, whose territory included my part of the county. "Sean," he said heartily after picking up on the first ring. "Are you finally taking me up on my offer?"

"No, Jimmy," I laughed. "But if I ever decide to move to your side of the fence, you'll be the first to know."

"Don't forget - I want first dibs," he added. "I could use an investigator like you on the team."

"Thanks."

"So, this isn't a social call then?"

"No. I've got a possible homicide down here; just a courtesy call, really."

"Seriously? In *Windeport*?"

"Yeah. I couldn't tell you the last one."

"Lovely. Do you need an assist?"

"Not yet," I said. "I've already got Heather working the scene, and the body is on the way to Augusta for a PM."

Jimmy paused. "Any other town in my beat and I'd muscle in, Sean," he said after a bit. "But your work speaks for itself. That task force gig in Bangor--"

"It was a lucky break," I interrupted, not wanting to go through the litany of cases I'd worked on, generally as a favor to a colleague in another part of the state. It was only partly altruistic; Windeport had quite happily charged for my time, too.

"Right," he chuckled. "You call if you need anything."

"Will do." I clicked off the phone and held it to my cheek for a long, thoughtful moment. I should have asked the Captain to take over the case, but not only did I fail to do that, I'd neglected to disclose I knew the deceased. While I was certainly within my purview to retain the case, it would have been wiser to have passed it up the food chain.

Tapping the edge of my iPhone on my cheek, I finally acknowledged to myself that something about the circumstances of Ingmar's death troubled me enough to want to get to the bottom of it personally. And yet, that little voice of reason in the back of my head was practically screaming that this was a bad idea. Normally I would listen to that voice.

Time would tell if I was making the right decision.

Three

Many hours after we had unceremoniously been yanked from the water by my deputies, and after a quick detour to retrieve my partner, I pulled up in the visitor lot behind the massive aquatics complex at the University of Eastern Maine. We were well beyond the normal practice time for our U. S. Masters Swimming club, but based on the time displayed on my dashboard, I had to assume the college team was well into their Monday morning sets. I grimaced as I stepped out of the SUV and fell into step beside Vasily. "Kids," I groaned.

"Just go into Chief mode," Vasily advised as I opened the door and allowed him to enter ahead of me. "They can smell fear."

"Can they now?" I smiled. "Good to know."

The short hallway connected to another door that had been propped open to the pool deck. I followed Vasily in and we worked our way around the controlled chaos a swim practice in session generated. I'd used the facility myself from the age of eight and was well acquainted with the two pools: one fifty-meter by twenty-five yard medium depth pool and a smaller, twenty-five meter by twenty-five meter diving well that doubled as the venue for the water polo team. Both pools were in use, with the larger set for fifty-meter long course. As we entered the men's locker room to retrieve the gear we'd left, I paused to watch a young diver launch himself off the ten-meter board and cleave the surface of the diving well with nary a splash.

I showered and changed into my semi-official work attire of a dark blue polo sporting the town seal and worn jeans, then waited for Vasily on the curb outside. For late October, it was shaping up to be a fairly warm day. If I'd had a bungalow like Ingmar, I'd have likely been running around performing those last-minute fall activities to prep for the coming winter: raking leaves, piling compost on the flower beds, wrapping the outdoor faucets against the first freeze. Thankfully, I owned an apartment and needed to do none of those.

My iPhone buzzed in my vest pocket and I retrieved it, smiling when I saw the name on the display. "Deidre," I said brightly. "How's Boston treating the love of my life?"

I heard the warm laugh of my girlfriend. "It would be better if my boyfriend were here," she replied.

"I know, and I'm forever sorry. Unfortunate luck that we would be hosting the Symposium the same week as your friend's wedding."

"I think you planned it," she said accusingly but in a good-natured way. "You've never liked Laura."

"Not true," I said, then paused. "I like Laura. I just can't stand her future husband."

"Honesty," she laughed again. "How refreshing."

"Was the rehearsal dinner last night?"

"Yes," Deidre replied.

Her best friend from college was marrying her longtime boyfriend in a no-holds-barred affair at the swanky Boston Harbor Hotel. My girlfriend was the maid of honor, and to be honest, was a bit upset that she was still a *maid*. We'd dated now for more than a decade, and while I loved her with all of my heart, for one reason or another, I'd not taken the next step and asked for her hand in marriage.

"Still coming back tomorrow afternoon?"

"Maybe," she replied. "I have the train tickets, but there is a fruit vendor here I want to talk to. If I decide to stop in, it would be late Tuesday or early Wednesday."

"I'm not sure your IGA will survive without you," I joked as Vasily emerged from the aquatics center.

"Likely true."

"Well, the sooner the better," I said. "I've missed you horribly."

"I know better," she laughed. "Hugs and kisses," she added before hanging up.

Vasily slid into the SUV, asking, "De?"

"Yeah," I said, thinking she had sounded a bit odd. "She's probably not back until Wednesday."

"Just as well," he offered as I started up the SUV and pulled out. "You'll be focused on this case anyway."

I started to say something and then paused. He was right, I did tend to become highly focused when we were working a case; Deidre had complained on more than a few occasions that I'd prioritized work over my personal life. Trying to shake off the thought, I asked: "Late breakfast? Then we can check in with Heather before heading over to the hotel."

Vasily put his head back on the seat and groaned. "We still have to do security for the keynote tonight?"

"I'm afraid so."

"This day just keeps getting better and better."

"Tell me about it."

Four

~~~~~~~~

We didn't normally provide security for events in Windeport, but the International Potato Symposium was a unique event drawing the best and the brightest in the field from all corners of the globe. Typically, it would be held in a destination city, but as one of the original founding members of the event, the University had put in a bid to host the fortieth anniversary edition. The scuttlebutt around the village was that they were also planning to trot out their premier researcher, Menard LaChance, who was rumored to be making a huge announcement.

For those involved in the world of potatoes, it was a big deal. For us, not so much. But the Village Council to whom I reported considered this a prime opportunity to show our little village could become a conference destination and help keep us going economically outside of the tourist season. Who was I to argue?

The Colonial was off Route One on the northeastern side of town, down a long, winding driveway lined by very tall, and incredibly old maple trees. During the spring and summer, it made the drive seem a bit claustrophobic, but in the fall and winter, barren and desolate. Someone at the hotel, presumably in the marketing department, had realized this and had hastened to wind strings of brightly lit LED lights through the empty branches and down the trunks, making it feel vaguely like a holiday you were unsure you hadn't already missed.

The hotel itself had been built in 1901 and was reputed to have been wired for electricity by Thomas Edison himself. It had two circular towers on either end of rectangular main building, seven stories tall and comprised of more than five hundred rooms. Now part of the Marriott chain, it had just wrapped a multimillion-dollar renovation that restored the luster to the grand old dame.

Vasily had been fairly quiet on the ride across town, trading texts with the two officers still at the bungalow; as I rounded the final corner and began to move up the circular drive that fronted the grand entrance, he cleared his throat. "Are you ever going to propose to her?"

I blinked. "De?"

"Yeah. Dude, you've been doing this dance with her for years," he said. I realized how tired he was at the insertion of his native Californian turn of phrase. Normally he hid his out-state-roots behind a remarkably effective Down East accent he'd perfected.

"We have," I agreed. "If you weren't my best friend, I'd be writing you up for insubordination just for asking."

"Lucky for me," he laughed. "Seriously, what's holding you back? Of all people, I can't believe it's the fear of commitment."

"It's not that," I agreed as we pulled up beneath the portico and I put the SUV into park. "Honestly? I don't know. We're comfortable as a couple, for sure, and I've just never felt the need to go further. Neither of us wants kids--"

At that, I saw Vasily's eyes widen. "She... *Deidre* told you that?"

"Yes...?" I said, seeing something in his expression. "What?"

"I don't want to talk out of school, Sean," he said cautiously.

"All right," I replied as we exited the vehicle. "No scratches this time, Phil," I said to the young valet that took my keys.

"Of course, Chief," he smiled as he slid into the driver's seat.

"And no, you can't turn on the lights, either."

As the smiling valet pulled the SUV away, I turned back to Vasily, who was tracking the progress of the SUV -- or, rather, the well-built valet who was behind the wheel. "Ah," I chuckled. "I wondered who you were seeing now. Isn't he a bit young for you?"

"Hey!" he cried at my observation, flushing slightly. "How did this get to be about *me*?" he asked as he fell into step beside me and we headed toward the grand revolving door.

"Nathan did you wrong," I offered. It had been a messy breakup between my friend and his ex, which is why he was currently crashing in my apartment. "I hope this isn't just a rebound lover."

He flushed a bit more. "Well, everyone deserves *some* fun from time to time," he said.

"Be careful," I advised as we pushed through to the main lobby.

"He's a placeholder," Vasily acknowledged, looking at me oddly. "Until the right guy comes along."

"Be careful," I repeated. "All right, spill it. What did you hear?"

"Overheard, actually," he said as he lowered his voice. Partly it was due to the sensitive nature of what he wanted to tell me, but the massive seven story atrium in the exact center of the hotel inspired muted conversation. "I was grabbing coffee at Patti's back in August and De was in line ahead of me. She'd just finished telling Patti how disappointed she was that you didn't want kids." He waited a beat. "Deidre was visibly upset, Sean; when she saw me, she quickly smiled, paid for her coffee and left."

"August?" I asked. "I think I remember her casually mentioning that her friend -- the one getting married this week? -- wants a large family." We were headed in the general direction of the reception desk and paused in front of a massive fountain. "I remember laughing and telling her I had no such illusions."

Vasily looked at me carefully. "Sean, you might want to talk to her again. *Seriously* talk to her. I think it might be an issue for her - and let's face it, neither one of you are getting any younger."

I blinked. Was that right? I thought back to that very morning; her side of the bed, untouched as it had been for days now; her side of the medicine cabinet mostly empty of her cosmetics, her portion of the closet holding a mere handful of cold-weather outfits. I'd been seeing it for a while now and hadn't really *seen* it. I blinked again. "Oh..." I said.

"It's your blind spot," Vasily offered. "Talk to her. Again."

I didn't have time to respond for a tall, older woman with a severe bun had seen us enter and was marching across the space. "Uh oh," I murmured.

Vasily turned in the direction I'd been looking. "Here comes the old battle axe."

Trying hard not to smile, I turned a bit toward Vasily. "Check in with Reception and see where Sylvia is," I asked. "I'll want her to join us when we take a look at the stage -- after I'm done with She Who Must Be Obeyed."

Eyes crinkled with laughter, Vasily simply nodded and left me to my fate. I turned toward the oncoming nor'easter and braced myself with the best smile I had in my catalog. "Doctor Bedard," I said with more warmth than I truly felt for the woman.

"Chief," she said, the word spit out as an epithet. "Where is it?"

I blinked, and realized I'd been doing a lot of that lately. "Where is *what*, exactly?"

Sighing like she was working with an undergrad struggling to understand the Krebs Cycle, she took a deep breath and tried again. "The document. The report. The research packet."

"Yvette, I haven't a clue what you're talking about. Would you care to fill me in a bit?"

Rolling her eyes, she gripped my elbow and forcefully propelled me toward a set of potted ferns, somehow mistaking their three-foot height as some sort of privacy screen. "He took all of it. We must have it back before the announcement tonight."

"Documents?" I said blankly. "What documents? What the hell are you talking about?"

The Dean of the College of Agriculture stepped back and reappraised me with her deep grey eyes. "Oh," she said after a moment. "Well, it's so typically Ingmar. Dead and still causing me trouble. I bet they're in his office."

I wasn't surprised that she already knew about Ingmar - it *was* a small town, after all. Bedard turned to go, dismissing me without dismissing me. This time, I nabbed her elbow. "Hang on a moment, Doctor," I said, spinning her on her heel. "Explain yourself."

Her expression was fiery, one that I knew she trained on her colleagues back at the college. "I don't explain myself to anyone," she said coldly,

"I know that," I retorted. "But I'm not just anyone. I'm the Chief of Police, and we're in the midst of an investigation. It sounds to me like you have information I need."

"Investigation?" she said. "Into what?

I arched an eyebrow.

"Right," she allowed. "You know Ingmar heads -- headed -- the Extension?" At my nod, she continued. "One of his roles is to vet any research that could be useful out in the field as it were."

"That's a standard practice?"

"For nearly a century," she replied. "Each researcher in our college who receives State or Federal funding is required to submit an overview of their work to him; if he determines -- determined -- we could use a partner in the county to test it, he'd request more details and then set up an experimental run."

"All right," I nodded, seeing where she was going, "and you're telling me something he reviewed recently has come up missing?"

"Yes," she said. "And we must have it back. I assumed he'd taken it out of spite."

That eyebrow of mine went up again. "Because...?"

Bedard had the good sense to look embarrassed. "I... cancelled his request to create the experiment agreement."

"I take it that's *not* standard?"

"Not normally, no." She softened her look a bit. "Seriously, Chief, I need that material back. It's proprietary."

"To...?

She looked a bit uncomfortable. "Right now, the University."

"Why do I hear a 'but' in there?"

"I can't discuss it any further," she said.

"I'll let that go for now," I said, "but I might want to know, later."

"Get it back," she said, "and we'll talk."

"What am I looking for?" I asked. "Thumb drive? DVD?"

Bedard actually laughed her rough laugh, reminding me that she was a two-pack-a-day smoker. "Ingmar? And tech? No, it'll be old fashioned paper. And lots of it."

"All right. How sensitive is this data? Are we talking top secret?"

"To us," she laughed again, sounding more like the dying gasps of some sort of ocean creature. "Bring it directly to me."

"I can't promise that, Yvette. My people are going to need to go through it."

"No," she said, eyes flashing. "It's--"

"Proprietary, I know. This isn't my first rodeo, Doctor. We'll protect it and keep the circle small."

"At least call me? When you find it?"

I nodded. "See you at the keynote tonight?" I asked, changing subjects.

Bedard lit up. "I wouldn't miss it. It's going to be our finest moment as an institution."

Trying hard not to laugh, considering there was a possible murder now tangentially linked to her big announcement, I replied: "I'll bet."

Five

The "new" conference center for the Colonial had been built in the late sixties and only modestly updated with the recent renovation. The architect had clearly been attempting to blend the Googie style that had been the rage at the time with the more modest Victorian look of the original hotel and had failed miserably. Still, passing through the space-age archway into the main concourse, I couldn't help but feel transported back in time to a different era.

One side of the massive hall was comprised of windows arched on three plains, held in by fluted beams of white trimmed in aluminum details. Oddly, even with that much bric-a-brac, the view of the ocean beyond was relatively unobstructed. The chandeliers were massive three-deck affairs of concentric circles above a huge lighted frosted globe. Opposite the glass was the main ballroom, the size of a football field and capable of becoming eight smaller meeting rooms. Each double door was trimmed in white neon lights. The checked industrial rug was new but seemed like it was original.

The space was hopping. Off to one side was a set of carnival-style booths for registration, with long lines of mostly bespectacled scientists waiting patiently for their turn. Clutches of people were chatting amiably in the rest of the available space, making navigating to the ballroom nearly impossible. Vasily and I managed to work our way to the center set of doors and slipped into the space.

The lights were fully on and chairs were still being brought in. We moved between the staff furiously working against deadline and toward the temporary stage that had been erected. Sylvia Gauthier was already there, iPad in one hand and talking on her earbuds.

"Not tomorrow. *Today*, Carl. I need the projector *today*." She paused and saw us as we came up the steps and smiled. "I don't care! We contracted with you months ago. If you must drive to Portland, you'd better get going."

"I wouldn't want to stand between her and anything," I whispered to Vasily.

"Me, either."

The call lasted a few more seconds and then she turned to us fully. "Guys," she said.

"I won't ask *why* you came to work today," I said, my hands indicating the stage. "But how are you doing?"

"Better," she said as she pulled out her earbuds. "It's still terrible, but not as shock-worthy as it was this morning. I run past his place every day."

I caught movement and saw that Vasily had quietly brought out his notebook. "You're two doors down, right?"

"Three," she said. "I bought out my parents when I moved back, but they still live with me when they're in Windeport for the summer."

"Ah," I smiled knowingly. "A double-edged sword, that."

Sylvia chuckled. "Well, I have it to myself for nine months of the year. It's not all bad."

"My father won't come back," I smiled. "Which I am *completely* okay with."

She looked at me. "Still haven't patched things up with him, have you?"

"No," I said, and quickly changed subjects. "We'll probably want to be stationed in different parts of the room tonight. I don't have a ton of spare bodies to give you - maybe four, max."

"That should be plenty," she said. "We've only got about eight hundred here, including the media. And it's not like we're hosting Intel." She smiled. "You're really only here to make that evil old goat happy."

"Bedard?" I laughed. "Yeah, she does seem rather insistent that the world will change after tonight."

Sylvia shook her head with laughter. "It's a friggin' potato conference! I highly doubt it."

"Hey, I'm all for better French fries," Vasily interjected.

Sylvia gave him an appraising glance. "Well, with a figure like that, you can *afford* to eat them."

"Hours in the gym and pool, ma'am," Vasily replied.

We spent another half hour or so going over the details of the evening, and then parted ways with Sylvia a bit after one o'clock. I tried to ignore the meaningful glances traded between Vasily and Phil as he returned the SUV to us and instead ruminated on the missing documents Bedard was so concerned about. As we drove toward Route One, I asked, "Do you have the inventory from the bungalow yet?"

"No," he said after checking his phone. "Why?"

"Bedard thinks Ingmar stole some paperwork from the University," I replied. "She said it would be obvious if we encountered it."

"Want me to call?"

"No, we'll go there and then his office at the U. Can you call Campus Police? Tell them to lock down Ingmar's office and lab? Just as a precaution."

"On it," he said.

I only vaguely heard his conversation, for my thoughts had moved on already. Normally, I would have begun plotting my search of the bungalow and trying to resolve why our two complete searches to date hadn't turned up anything. But instead, our conversation with Sylvia had me thinking of Father. We'd not talked since the Fourth of July, and even that had been the briefest of brief chats. He'd never really recovered from losing Mom to breast cancer; it had been barely six months from when we buried her to him selling the pharmacy and decamping to Sarasota.

Part of me also suspected I was still in the proverbial doghouse for not following time-honored Colbeth tradition and taking over the pharmacy from him as he had from his father, as had been done on down the Colbeth line for nearly a century and a half. Being a pharmacist had never been part of my career path, but for Father, it had been a flat-out betrayal of family. Combined with the death of Mom, things had gotten seriously chilly between us.

Heather Graham was packing the last of her tools into the back of her van when we pulled to the curb behind her. "I thought it was going to take her longer," I said as I turned off the SUV.

"Same here," Vasily replied as we exited the sedan.

Heather was peeling off the paper jumpsuit she'd been wearing and looked up at our approach. "Chief," she nodded.

"Finished?"

"For now," she said. "I'm going to grab some lunch and then do a final round of photos. But to be honest, there's not much here. All but two rooms are empty."

I nodded; we'd seen that too. "It looked to us like he might have been thinking of selling."

"Yeah, but where are the boxes?" she asked.

I smiled. "True," I nodded to Vasily.

"I'll check the self-storage units in town," he said.

"Oh, this is for you," she continued, pulling something out of the back of the truck. "I was going to drop it by the station, but since you're here…"

She handed me a small plastic bag, which held a single rather deformed bullet. "Where was it?"

"Right where you thought," she replied. "About at the height his head would have been when the shot went through him, embedded in the drywall."

"Just one?"

"Just one."

"Prints?"

"One set in most places, but I found a second set on the doorknob to the carport."

"That's it?" I said, incredulous.

"Yeah. This guy must have had a monastic life. No visitors at all."

"Maybe," I arched an eyebrow at Vasily. "You didn't happen to run across anything looking like research, did you? Piles of paper? Big yellow envelope?"

Heather looked thoughtful for a moment. "Not that I recall," she said, "but I can cross check my list of items against what your officers came up with. In case it's suddenly gone missing."

I looked to Vasily. "A good precaution. And no gun, either?"

"No." she said, "I'm not an expert, but from the looks of that bullet, you're looking for something along the lines of a standard issue Glock."

"Available everywhere," I muttered.

"Exactly." She closed the doors to the van. "By the way, any idea why he had those five-gallon bottles of water?"

"I don't follow," I frowned.

She looked at us, dumfounded. "Guys... there's no water cooler in that house."

Six

As we drove toward campus for the second time that day, I tried hard not to think about the fact we had missed that simple item. It now made the tableau in the truck even more suspect. "How did we miss that?" I asked.

"It was early?" Vasily offered. "Or we weren't truly considering foul play."

"It's the latter," I sighed as we turned onto Route One and headed southwest. Most of the shops along the main drag had closed for the season - the ones that were still operating. More and more of the retail spots were like the old pharmacy and had been vacant for more than a few years. It was a sad commentary on the decline in our local population - or the rise in the big box retailers that had perched just outside of the village limits.

I pulled rank and parked in the red zone outside of Tavantis Hall, the headquarters for the College of Agriculture. Two junior officers from Campus Police met us at the sidewalk. "Chief," the taller of the two said. "I'll take you up."

I started to thank him when my iPhone buzzed. Pulling it out, I saw Father's cell number and tried to keep the shocked expression off my face. "Vasily, go ahead up."

"Right."

As they entered, I answered. "Father?" I asked. "Is everything--"

"I can't believe you've let that immoral disgrace of a human being into our *home*, let alone allow him to stay with you. Overnight."

I had to hold the phone out and turn down the volume. I wasn't surprised he'd found out Vasily was staying with me again - he still had plenty of friends who reported back to him on a regular basis - nor did I particularly care what his feelings about Vasily's supposed "chosen" lifestyle were. "Vasily is going through a rough patch, Father," I said rather curtly. "And I am his best friend. I'm frankly a bit too busy to deal with your homophobia today. Get to the point, please."

"I'm selling the building," Father said triumphantly. "You need to be out by November 15."

"You're... *what*?"

"Sold it, actually. Someone from out-of-state who'll put God knows what back. Doesn't matter. Start packing and get the Hell out of my home."

I choked back the next ten irate things that came to mind and went for number eleven. "We had an understanding, Father. I've been paying you rent all these years, which was part of our rent-to-own agreement."

"Don't worry, I've held it all in escrow. You'll get your rent back. Just get the Hell out and take your boyfriend with you."

That made me raise both eyebrows. "You do realize I'm dating Deidre, right? That she's been living with me for more than a year?"

"Out. By the fifteenth." And with that, he hung up.

I found myself standing there with the dead phone to my ear, wondering how much odder the day could get. Having to add "finding a new home" to my to-do list was not something I'd anticipated. I was about to turn and follow Vasily in when the phone buzzed again. "Hello?"

"Sean, it's Heather."

"That was a short lunch."

"Doesn't take long to snarf down a lobster roll," she laughed. "Look, that package you were looking for?"

"Yeah," I said, trying not to sound excited. "Did you find it?"

"No. But I did find one of those old-school Postal Service tracking forms. I'd seen it before, of course, but after we talked, I took a closer look at it. Whatever he mailed, it was heavy."

"Like a ton of documents?"

"Like a ton of documents."

"Where did it go?"

"The address looks like Boston. I'll snap a photo on my phone and text it to you."

"Awesome work, Heather. Lobster is on me tonight."

"Thanks," she laughed, "but I'll take a raincheck. I'm going back after I'm done. You'll have my full report plus the photos by Wednesday."

"Great."

I hung up again and this time made my way to Ingmar's office. Just as when I'd been an undergraduate, it was still on the fourth floor, a small rectangle of a space that barely held his old wooden desk and an overstuffed bookcase that ran end-to-end. Vasily had wedged himself into the space and was flipping through stacks and stacks of documents on his desk; hundreds more were piled around on the floor. He was frowning when I poked my head in.

"It might be in Boston," I said without preamble. "Heather found a tracking postcard at the bungalow."

"That sort of makes sense," Vasily said as he looked up. "If he was trying to keep it away from Bedard, maybe he mailed it to a friend or colleague in Boston."

I leaned against the door jamb. "You know, this can't be the only copy of the research," I mused. "No one uses paper today. It had to have been printed from something."

"True."

"So, the only reason he mailed a copy was to keep it outside of Bedard's orbit. Off campus."

"To try and spoil the announcement tonight? That seems like a stretch."

"Yeah - maybe not. Bedard kept insisting this research is 'proprietary.'"

Vasily's eyes widened. "You're not thinking he pulled some sort of Wikileaks escapade?"

I laughed. "I suspect the Pentagon Papers would be a more appropriate analogy if my hunch is right. Still, let's dig through this mess for a bit just to make sure he didn't misplace it. Otherwise, we're off to the land of soft pretzels and microbrews."

"Sam Adams is *not* a microbrew."

"Says you." I thought for a moment. "I'm going to see if I can track down an admin, actually. It would be nice to know what we're looking for. *Someone* printed it for him since there's no printer in this office - let alone a workstation."

Vasily nodded and I retraced my steps to the department office I'd passed on my way up. Pushing through the double-glass doors, I found a beautiful African American woman dressed in purple tones and sporting tasteful streaks of white in her afro seated behind the standard issue desk. An undergrad was standing in front of her, shifting weight from one leg to the other.

"No," the woman said. "There is a GPA requirement for that course, and you don't meet it."

"But I *need* the course!" the young woman pleaded. "It's necessary for medical school!"

"Honey, I don't care if you need it to get your Driver's License. You're not getting in until you get that GPA up."

"Miss Thompson--"

"Don't 'Miss Thompson' me young woman," she said, glaring over her glasses. "You were warned two semesters ago." Her look softened slightly. "Look," she said, as she produced a folded pamphlet. "Take this down to Hailey 209 and ask for Maddie. Then come back and see me."

"All right," the student said, taking the paper and then dejectedly walking past me to the doors.

"Barb, you've still got the touch," I laughed.

"Sean!" she cried and, in an instant, had managed to get out from behind the desk and envelop me in a massive hug. "How the hell are you? You never call."

"Sorry," I shrugged. "You haven't aged a bit."

"Flatterer," she laughed, slapping me on the bicep. "Truth be told, I'm feeling old these days. The kids are getting younger and younger." She stepped back. "Tie the knot with that redhead of yours?"

I shook my head. "De? Not yet."

"What the Hell are you waiting for?" she asked, eyes wide. "You've loved her from the get-go."

I rolled my eyes. "Anyway," I started as she moved back behind her desk. "I'm looking for some information."

"Are you, now?" she smiled.

"You've already heard about Ingmar?"

"Yeah," she frowned. "Odd man, but I loved him to pieces. All of us did."

"We were joking earlier about the little exam racket he had going. Was he still--"

"Yes," she laughed. "Although the price had gone up - $10.50. And he started to accept Apple Pay this year."

"Ingmar?" I replied, eyes wide. "He doesn't even have a computer!"

Barbara chuckled, which for her was something of a full-body affair. Wiping tears from her eyes, she pointed to a small machine on the counter. "He didn't do it," she gasped between chuckles.

"Well, I guess you can teach an old professor new tricks," I smiled.

"Not always," she replied a bit more soberly. "I still had to print a hard copy of his daily schedule."

"About that," I started. "Were you the one that printed out the research that he reviewed? For the Extension part of his duties?"

"Hell yeah," she chortled. "I have a whole closet of paper just for *that* one task."

"I can imagine. Any chance you know what the last few were that he saw?"

"I can do better," Barb said as she turned to her computer. "Believe it or not, there's an actual database with this information."

"Modern marvel, that," I laughed.

"Let me change the query a bit... and... there," she said as the laser printer to her side burst into life. Turning, she plucked two pages from the printer and scanned the text. "Looks like he was reviewing ten different projects," she reported as she handed me the sheets. "Top one is the most recent."

I quickly scanned the paper myself. "Disease resistant potato... kale that can grow in less temperate climates... easier to digest corn... sugar cane that can be used as fuel." I looked up at Barb. "These are all ongoing projects here at the U?"

"Yes sir." She waited a beat before adding, "Ongoing might be a bit optimistic. Ingmar had been having trouble finding funds for more than a few researchers; Doctor LaChance was the main beneficiary of his efforts."

My eyes went back to the list. Given that Bedard was worried about something getting out before the keynote at the Symposium... "Can you download this first one?"

"Sure," she said, sliding open a drawer and pulling out a flash drive.

"This is the part where I tell you Bedard had warned me that the research is proprietary..."

"Screw Doctor Uptight," Barb laughed. "The taxpayers of the state paid for this research. I think, as a taxpayer, you're within your rights to view these materials."

I couldn't help but laugh. "Barb, you've just brightened my day."

"It's what I do, sweetheart," she smiled as she handed me the drive. "It's what I *live* for."

Seven

I left Vasily at the station and started to drive back to the apartment to grab a shower and a quick bite of dinner before heading in for our duty at the Symposium. But at the turn onto Route One, I abruptly changed my mind and adjusted course. There were a handful of real estate agencies in town, but only one of note. If Ingmar were selling his bungalow, my guess was that he'd have talked to Elaine West.

Her office was housed in an even older brick block at the far end of the main drag. As I pulled into a parking spot in front, I could see the lights were still on and one blond head still there in the main office suite. Elaine caught my headlights as they raked across the plate glass window and waved to me; a moment later, she met me at the door. "Sean," she smiled. "What's up? Ready to sell the pharmacy building?"

I frowned as I followed her into the open space; small desks were in the main area, with glass-enclosed offices against the far wall, likely for sealing the deal in private. "Father's already taken care of that, actually," I said lightly.

"Oh," she replied as a look of disappointment crossed her face. "That's too bad. It's the second commercial spot I missed out on this month."

"Really?" I said. "I didn't think the market was that great at the moment."

"It's not," she allowed. "But pharmacies and grocery stores tend to be in prime locations."

My smile froze. "Grocery stores?"

Elaine flushed. "Oh, Sean..." she said slowly. "I thought... Deidre didn't tell you?"

"No," I said, my thoughts spinning slightly.

"I assumed you were here for the paperwork she asked for. My mistake."

"Not a problem," I said breezily. "Actually, I was wondering if you were listing Ingmar Pelletier's bungalow?"

Relieved to be talking about anything other than her apparent faux paus, Elaine brightened. "Actually I am. Unfortunately, I'm not likely to get the price he was asking originally."

"Why not?"

She looked uncomfortable again. "Well... given what happened to the last owner..."

"Ah," I smiled. "Death has a way of messing with valuation."

"Exactly."

"Why was he selling, exactly? Do you know? I wasn't aware he was thinking of retiring."

"You know what? I never asked. I assumed he was going to Florida. That's where most of my older clients head."

"Do you have the price sheet?" I asked. "For my files," I added.

"Sure," she said. Elaine moved to a desk in the far corner of the open office and flipped through some files, ultimately returning with a one-sheet. "I'll be updating this tomorrow with a new price, but the essentials are all here."

"Are you staging the house?" I asked. "I couldn't help but notice how empty it is."

"No," she frowned. "He told me he'd sold off just about everything. A few key pieces of furniture would have been nice, actually. But again, I thought he was downsizing for a move."

"He may well have been," I said. "Did he ask for any agents in Florida?"

"No," she said, scratching her chin. "No, he didn't." She looked at me.

"Normally they do, and I have a handful in several parts of the state I refer people to all the time."

"Could one of your staff have given them out?"

"Maybe," she nodded.

"If you don't mind giving me the list, we'll reach out and see if we can confirm any contact."

"Of course. But if he went with someone else, you might be left doing a property record search."

"I've done plenty of those," I laughed. "Thanks," I added as I turned to go.

"See you at the party?" she asked.

I tried not to roll my eyes. "Charlie already told you I was coming?"

"Oh yes," she smiled. "I think the entire village is looking forward to seeing our very proper Chief of Police let his hair down."

Laughing, I ran a hand through my hair, tousling it up a bit. It wasn't hard - I'd inherited something of a curl from my mother, which required an unseemly amount of gel just to tame into something close to a "professional" look. Add to that years of chlorine damage and letting it "down" was the most unlikely outcome possible. "I fear everyone will be disappointed."

"I doubt that."

Back in the SUV, I glanced at the box still sitting on the passenger seat before starting it up. I'd been roped into attending the town's official Halloween party as part of our campaign for safe trick-or-treating, and my cousin had convinced me to come in costume. Having not dressed up for Halloween since the age of ten, I wasn't thrilled with the idea but bowed to the considerable pressure (and sheer determination) Charlie had trained on me. It didn't hurt that I'd be able to hang with my two nieces - perhaps the only kids in town I felt comfortable to be about.

I pulled away from the curb and headed home, trying hard not to think about the costume in the box. It had been an academic exercise before the physicality of the box reminded me I'd have to go through with it. The things we do for family...

I turned left and away from the ocean onto a side street beside the empty pharmacy and then right into a small parking lot behind the ancient brick building. As I was the only tenant these days, I had my pick of spots - though Vasily's Camaro was in his normal spot. Seeing it brought my earlier conversation with my father front and center, and I could feel the roil of anger in my gut. That was also a reminder I'd not had anything solid to eat since our late breakfast. Grabbing the box from the seat, I locked the SUV and shuffled keys to unlock the door to the stairwell leading to the second-floor residence.

The stairwell was tiny, as appropriate to eighteenth century construction, but widened to a nicely sized landing in front of the ornate door to the apartment. That door was unlocked per our custom, and I moved through the short hallway that led into the long living room that paralleled Route One. "Vasily?"

"In the kitchen."

I dropped my keys and the Amazon box on the small banquet that had been a favorite of my mother and rounded the corner of the hallway. It was an open family room concept that Father had created in the late eighties, with the kitchen against the far wall with a small half-wall acting as a both a view break and a breakfast bar. Vasily was on the other side, staring at a pot on the gas stove.

"You know what they say about watched pots..." I laughed.

"Don't get me started," he chuckled. "Hungry? I'm doing spaghetti. The deli had some of those prosciutto meatballs on hand and they called out to me."

"I won't refuse."

"Ready in about fifteen then." He paused for a moment. "Oh - Caitlyn handed me that folder on the ledge when I was at the station. She managed to get ahold of Darryl at the Post Office and did a back trace on the tracking number from that postcard."

"She called Darryl? Why didn't she just look it up on the website?"

"Ingmar didn't pay for tracking, just a signature on delivery."

"Oh," I nodded. "But Darryl would be able to look at their internal records."

"Exactly."

I flipped open the folder and saw a Dun and Bradstreet report for one *American Journal of Potato Research*, located on Franklin Street in downtown Boston. I knew the spot well, for my maternal grandfather had worked in that same building when it had been the headquarters for New England Telephone. "Pack your bags, Detective. It's off to Boston in the morning."

"One step ahead of you," he laughed.

"All right," I replied as I headed down the only other hallway. Two master suites filled that space with a smaller room I used as my home office. I found myself unwittingly cataloging how I would need to pack everything up. Pausing at the entrance to the den, I looked at the bookcases full of books - not just mine, but those of my parents that Father hadn't taken when he'd moved out. Turning back and looking down toward Vasily at the far end, happily humming to himself as he worked through the kitchen, it dawned on me that other than those years I'd been in a dorm or travelling with the U.S. National Swim Team, I'd never lived anywhere else.

Entering my room, my eyes fell on Deidre's side of the bed; between what Vasily had told me that morning, and finding out that Deidre had sold the IGA, I was starting to see a pattern that I'd likely been ignoring. Willfully.

I put on my Chief of Police persona and started to look at the room as if it were an investigation, finally seeing the clues Vasily had rightly told me I was blind to. Sliding the closet door open, the two sweaters that remained were ones I had given her for our ski outings to Sunday River; a few weeks ago, she'd been complaining how tiny the closet had been, and then it had been bulging over into my side. There was a strange physicality to the empty space on the shelf above where her suitcase and overnight bag had once been. Moving to the attached master bath, I popped open the medicine cabinet and found the cosmetics that remained were near to or had expired. No shampoo, no deodorant. And, perhaps most tellingly, no toothbrush.

For who takes a toothbrush when you have a travel-sized one in your overnight bag?

Sitting on the closed lid of the toilet, I found it hard to believe that less than a week ago, she'd been here in this space with me, much as she had been for years. We'd been tangled together in the sheets of the bed, breathless after making love to each other; I'd surprised her in the shower the morning after, and if I closed my eyes, could still feel the hot water as it cascaded over the two of us.

Now I knew, it was the day she left.

Had I become so comfortable in our relationship that I'd taken her for granted? That we would always be together? Staring at the tile on the bathroom floor, I started to think at least one of us had. Signs had been everywhere, and subconsciously or not, I'd ignored them.

I pulled out my iPhone and was tempted to call her; part of me wondered if her earlier call had been an initial attempt to tell me she wasn't coming back. Yet she had lied to me instead - not, perhaps, to protect my feelings, but more to avoid the acrimony or recriminations. Then again, she didn't know me very well if she thought that would be how I'd handle things. Rolling the phone in my hands, I decided this was going to be handled best in person. And since we were likely off to Boston tomorrow, I'd have the opportunity.

Taking a chance, I punched up Deidre's phone number and dialed. She picked up after the second ring. "Sean?" she said, loudly. There was a lot of background noise. "What's wrong?"

"Nothing," I said, trying to sound cheerful. "Say, are you still going to be in Boston another day?" I asked, innocently forgetting she'd originally told me she'd be home on Wednesday.

The pause was nearly imperceptible. "Looks like it. Hang on, let me get somewhere quieter."

I waited a moment. After a fashion, the background noise decreased by more than half. "That's better," I said.

"They have these old phone booths in the lobby," she explained. "Why do you ask?"

"I've got to come down to follow up on a lead in an investigation I'm working," I said. "I don't know how long I am going to be, so I'll probably overnight at the Harbor or the Marriott. I thought we could catch dinner, if you're still there," I added, wondering why I'd phrased it just that way.

There was a long, long pause. Then, with what sounded like forced cheerfulness, she replied. "That would be wonderful! Text me when you get here, and we'll decide on a time."

"Will do," I said. "See you tomorrow, my love," I said automatically.

"Until tomorrow."

I clicked off and sat there, on the toilet lid, sorting through my turbulent emotions, totally uncertain of my next move. For a trained investigator, that was perhaps the scariest part of all. Our trip to Boston was shaping up to be interesting in more ways than one. The longer I sat there, though, the more one thing started to become clear.

Slowly, I stood and moved into the bedroom.

"Alexa," I said, and was rewarded by seeing my small internet device light up with a blue ring. "Play *Sad Songs* by Elton John."

As the music filled the room, I yanked the trash bag out of the bin by the bed and proceeded to clean out the reminders of my life that could have been before heading back to Vasily and dinner.

Eight

I took up position backstage. The receiver in my ear and microphone in the cuff of my blazer had me feeling like one of those Secret Service agents, sans sunglasses. It wasn't a feeling I enjoyed. I figured my dirty blond curls would likely have prevented me from being cast as one in a movie or television show; on screen, they always had perfectly coifed hair, square jaws, and bulging biceps. I had none of those attributes, but then again with my relentless Masters Swimming routine, my biceps weren't exactly *bad*, either. I might have even still had something of a six-pack, too, though in truth my abs weren't what they had been at the Olympics. Age catches up with everyone eventually.

It was evident that the Colonial had hired professional event planners to assist with the Symposium. There was a flotilla of techs clad in unrelieved black dashing to-and-fro, responding to needs that were ever changing. The actual evening session had been going on for about fifteen minutes; the current president of the association was speaking, going over the agenda for the next few days and then trying to build up enthusiasm for the keynote. Given the rustling I was hearing backstage, I could tell he was doing a poor job of it.

Parting the curtain, I looked out across the darkened ballroom. Surprisingly, it was standing room only, though given how courteously the scientists were behaving, you'd have thought the space was empty. Academia was in an entirely different orbit than reality, I decided, one with its own quirks and language. You'd never have seen a crowd this quiet at a Police convention.

"Position report," I said quietly.

"Quiet in the rear," Vasily promptly reported back.

"Lobby is quiet," Officer Napier reported.

"I've got an issue in the green room, Chief," Officer Smart said, her voice a bit animated. "I could use an assist from a higher authority."

"On my way," I said. "Vasily, take the stage?"

"Only if I can do my standup routine."

"Oh, this is the proper audience for that," I chuckled quietly. "They're already asleep; you won't harm them at all."

"Ouch," he replied.

I made my way further into the temporary wings of the stage, down the riser steps and into a back hallway of the conference facility. The green rooms were really nothing more than two closets that had been hurriedly converted to a hangout space for the speakers; I pushed into the room to find Lydia standing between Yvette Bedard and the keynote speaker, Menard LaChance. Bedard looked like she was about to blow a major blood vessel in her forehead while LaChance seemed to have this oddly dazed expression.

Lydia relaxed upon my entrance. "Chief," she said, her cheeks flaming with a bit of embarrassment. "I tried to stop her from coming in, but she pushed right past me."

I refrained from pointing out that only one of them had a gun.

"Yvette," I said, "generally speaking, we follow the orders of uniformed officers."

"I am a VIP at this conference. Hell, I *paid* for this conference. I can go where I damn well please."

"No," I said firmly. "I'm going to have to ask you to leave."

"Chief --"

"*Now*, Doctor." I took her by the arm and moved the two of us toward the door.

"Let me *go*," she said angrily. "I have some last-minute notes for Menard that he must incorporate into the speech he's about to give."

"I'll bet you do," I said. "You can provide that to me. Out there," I emphasized with a nod of my head.

"It's okay," LaChance suddenly said. "And she's not here to give me notes. She's about to accuse me of allowing Ingmar full access to my research without having her approval in advance."

"I was *not*," Bedard spluttered, but the truth was in the anger behind her eyes.

"Yes, you were," LaChance said simply. "And for the millionth time, Yvette, I didn't. Aside from the material I was obligated to share for the Extension's review."

"I have records, Menard," Bedard said coldly. "The database shows a full packet was created and downloaded. And we know Ingmar couldn't have done it himself."

"I don't know what to tell you," LaChance said. "Other than I've got to go on stage," he added when one of the black-clad stagehands appeared at the door to the green room.

"We'll talk later," Bedard promised as LaChance moved past her.

"Of that I am certain," he smiled vaguely and disappeared.

I turned to Bedard. "Really? Before he gives the keynote that will change the world?"

She had the good sense to look a little chagrined. "I thought if I caught him unawares, he'd spill his guts," she said.

"It doesn't work like that in the real world. Not like what you see on television."

"Clearly," she said. "But I'm still convinced he had a hand in getting the full data to Ingmar."

I decided it would be best not to mention I had a sense of who had done it - or that I was reasonably certain where the packet was currently. "Leave the investigation to us, Doctor. It's what we do."

"Keep me informed," she commanded and then, back straight, marched out into the hallway.

"She's really something, isn't she, sir?"

I laughed for the first time that evening. "Yes, yes she is."

Nine

I reclaimed my position backstage and sent Vasily to his original post just as the emcee announced LaChance. To very polite, almost golf-fan-like clapping, I watched LaChance as he stepped through the curtain, only to step back again to have his lapel microphone attached. I took that moment to exit backstage myself and stand just below the temporary platform, eyes scanning the crowd.

"Thank you," LaChance said as the polite clapping faded. "My friends and colleagues, today may well stand out as one of the most important days in our field - pun intended," he laughed, and the crowd joined him for a moment.

I turned more toward the stage, for this was not the same LaChance I'd seen in the green room a few minutes earlier. *That* LaChance had the typical air of a researcher with a tenuous grasp on reality; *this* LaChance was some sort of motivational speaker.

The curtains had closed behind him, and a massive white screen had descended from the ceiling. As the logo for the University lit up, LaChance continued. "Today, my friends, I announce the arrival of something that will radically change the future of potato agriculture."

"Dear Lord," I heard from Vasily as the crowd erupted in what felt more like a rock-star cheer - radically different than the polite crowd of ten seconds ago. "Permission to check out?"

"Denied," I laughed. "Give the man his moment."

And it was a moment LaChance was reveling in. Smiling as he took the clicker from the podium, he started to walk the stage, waiting for the crowd to calm down before speaking once more. "Friends," he said, pausing on the far edge of the stage. "Consider the potato."

The screen changed to show the typical specimen you would find in any grocery store; oddly, my mind immediately continued onward to the IGA that was no longer Deidre's. With difficulty, I forced my attention back to LaChance.

"Hardy in its own right, the potato has a veritable armada of bacterium, viruses and other parasites pummeling it's defenses each season. Year after tortuous year, these invaders continue to find new and ever more creative ways to infect or otherwise render non-harvestable this important crop."

"Get to the French fries," Vasily whispered.

"Hush."

The slide changed to show something of a timeline of potato breakthroughs, and I took that moment to scan the crowd again. I recognized the classic tactic: much like a good prosecutor, LaChance was setting up the audience for whatever discovery he was about to announce.

"Through a crude form of trial and error, my predecessors in this field dug up a few varieties more resistant than most," he continued, letting the audience laugh at what I thought was a stretch, pun-wise. "More importantly, perhaps, they stumbled on a few that were ideal for the climate we experience in these latitudes."

I happened to catch Yvette Bedard at that moment; the expression on her face told me she was taking that last comment personally if the quiver of her lip was an indicator. I wondered if I should offer LaChance protective custody after the speech was over.

"I want to pause here for a moment to recognize someone who was instrumental in ensuring my research was able to be completed." The slide changed to show the professional headshot of Ingmar Pelletier, presumably from the University's website. He looked far younger than the man I pulled out of the back of the pickup less than twelve hours ago.

"We lost Ingmar today," LaChance said quietly. "But in his role as

Associate Dean for Research, he managed to come up with the seed funding to get my radical idea going; when it showed promise, he advanced me money from the Extension service long before any results were available to back his bet." He paused again. "Ingmar was a friend - to me, to the University, and to the industry."

I hadn't been aware of Pelletier's role in the project and filed it away.

After a longer pause, he added, "He'll be missed."

The screen changed again as LaChance walked to the opposite side of the stage. "When I started this journey, DNA technology was still in its infancy. Creating and then refining the massive database of DNA we would need to mine became easier, though, with the advent of cloud computing; AI-infused sequencers eventually replaced the gels we were running manually, speeding up our runs. It was nearly three years before we were even able to begin the process of crafting the potato that my team *knew* was out there, waiting to be discovered."

A flash and then a photo straight out of a science-fiction horror movie appeared, the audience gasping at its appearance. "We had our first setback, and then our next," he said, clicking through a series of photos that looked like anything but a potato. "For two long years, every combination that seemed able to create a solid root crop turned out to be another dead end. Thousands of seedlings were grown, tediously, only to produce monstrosities such as these."

LaChance paused on one specimen and laughed. "I suppose it wasn't a total loss. This beauty, though ugly, turned out to need one-fifth the water of a standard specimen."

I found myself mesmerized by the presentation. No stranger to science myself, given the advancements that had been made in my own field, I found it incredible that someone had dedicated their life to what I'd always thought of as a commodity. That thing you had as a side dish at dinner. Nothing special - and yet, maybe it was.

LaChance clicked and the screen shifted to his final slide. A nearly perfectly petite white-purple flower appeared; beside it sat a very ordinary looking potato. "This, my friends, is the result of ten years of arduous research. Relentless testing by my lab has proven this potato to be resistant to even the worst virus my colleagues in the Biology department can engineer. What's more? This particular variety has its own version of a human white blood cell, making it capable of detecting an infection of *any* sort and capably defeat it without the aid of any chemicals, natural or otherwise."

"And," he said, pausing almost like a septuagenarian version of Steve Jobs, "there's one more thing. It's perfectly safe for human consumption."

The crowd erupted in rapturous cheering, and despite not completely understanding the science, I felt compelled to appreciate their admiration. It certainly sounded like a super-potato. And now I understood why Bedard was so keen on keeping the research to a small circle of people.

"There's no way in Hell I would ever eat that," Vasily said.

I laughed as the crowd continued to cheer, adding, "You might be right. This French fry might just eat you."

Ten

We arrived in Boston just ahead of the lunch hour, and I spontaneously decided to splurge and checked us into the Ritz-Carlton on Avery. I knew I was still in the early part of my budget year, though most of my travel to that point had been priced into the numerous consulting gigs Vasily and I had already completed. And it wasn't splurging, exactly, since my badge had garnered me the significant Government Discount. Still, any chance to stay at a five star was worth it - especially one that had been the fictional setting for some of my favorite Robert B. Parker novels.

It also didn't hurt it was equidistant between the Boston Harbor Hotel (where Deidre was ostensibly staying) and the location of our appointment at two that afternoon with the editor of the *Journal*. Both were an easy walk or a quick trip on the subway.

We dropped our gear in the room and more for ease than anything else, took a table at the Artisan Bistro. The space was as ornate as the hotel it was housed in, with gold trim just about everywhere you looked and waitstaff dressed in modest but expensively tailored uniforms. I tried to ignore the prices on the lunch menu, knowing it would be a bit of a challenge to get it through on my travel per diem. I was considering the choice between steak salad and steak proper when Vasily spoke.

"You're talking to De today," he said. It was more of an observation than anything else.

"Yeah," I replied. "I figured since we were here, I'd have dinner with her." I slipped my phone out and saw that she had yet to reply to my text message that I was in Boston. "Maybe."

"I'll assume you will," he smiled, "and see if one of the scalpers out there has tickets to *Hamilton*."

My eyebrows went up. "I didn't know it had gotten to Boston finally."

"It's been everywhere else, for sure," he said as he folded his menu and pushed a stray hair behind an ear. "But it opened here about a week ago."

"It won't be cheap," I said.

"I won't pay face value," he smiled.

That concerned me. "Be careful," I advised. "I don't want to have to explain why you were in Mass General with a knife wound."

"I will," he smiled again. "Look," he continued after we placed our order. "I didn't know how to tell you about Deidre."

"You... knew?"

"Sean, you are the best investigator I know, but like I said, you have a huge blind spot for your personal life. The whole village knew she'd packed up and left. The sale of the IGA wasn't a secret."

I blinked. "In the future, a gentle heads up would be nice."

Vasily flushed slightly. "It wasn't my place, dude," he said, lowering his head to hide his face. "And I wasn't sure how you'd react." He grew a bit quieter. "I... also didn't want you to think I had... ulterior motives... in telling you what I knew."

I thought it best to take a sip of the iced tea the waiter had brought to me, for it allowed me the extra moment to digest what my best friend was saying. Vasily had been my closest friend since we were in college together and been with me on the National Team for Olympics. The entire reason he'd enrolled at the University had been quite simple: after he'd come out to his parents, they'd kicked him to the curb. Having expected that, Vasily had accepted a scholarship from the school furthest from his intolerant parents in Orange County. Maine wasn't exactly known for being open and affirming, but the University *had* been, and he'd grown to love Windeport enough that he'd stayed after graduation.

"Vasily," I said cautiously, "I would never think that."

He looked up at me, slight relief on his face. "Cool."

I paused when the waiter returned to refill our drinks; it wasn't lost on me that he took a little longer with Vasily. Smiling, I realized it provided me an opening. "What is it with you?" I asked.

Nonplussed, he flushed a bit. "It must be the hair," he laughed nervously. "It gives me an exotic flair, especially when I have a tan."

"Or that Greek God body of yours."

He smiled wider. "You noticed. How sweet."

That made me chuckle. "You have no idea. No matter how much I work out, I just don't have the same body type as you and could never measure up. But it doesn't prevent me from appreciating something I can never have." I waited a beat. "Man or woman, for that matter."

Vasily nodded slowly, a slight look of surprise on his face. "Good to know," he smiled slightly.

When the waiter appeared with our entree, Vasily gave him a warm smile; he looked back to me after we'd each been served. "Are you sure you don't want company when you meet with her?"

"No," I said as considered my dish. "I need to do this alone. But I appreciate the offer."

"Deidre could still change her mind," he said with his usual optimism. "Stranger things have happened."

I shook my head. "I don't need you false hope. To be honest, what I want most is for her to be happy; if that's with someone else, I'll get over it. Eventually."

"Maybe with the help of someone new," he smiled, and then changed the subject to the off season moves the Red Sox had started to make.

After lunch, we decided to walk to our appointment and made our way across the city to Franklin street. It was hard for me to reconcile that we were a day from Halloween, given that the lunchtime temperature in Boston was in the mid-seventies; being New England, I suspected I'd be bundled up against an early freeze tomorrow at the village

Halloween Party. The corner of Franklin that the *Journal* had its office was part of the Financial District and sported multiple high rises, some with names of organizations I no longer recognized.

The old New England Telephone building still housed parts of its successor organization, Verizon Communications. But since the company was essentially now based in New York, the extra office space had been subleased. Still, the building itself was incredibly representative of the golden age of telecommunications, with nifty Art Deco motifs evocative of communications. I wondered if any of the college-aged kids we were passing on the sidewalk had any sense of the history the sandstone-sided building represented, or of the tech that had once dominated our lives.

Passing through the gilded doors to the lobby, we located the floor housing the *Journal* and went to the appropriate bank of elevators. A few moments later, we were stymied by a mousy man with a thin mustache seated behind a semi-circular reception desk.

"Do you have an appointment?" he asked in a high, nasally voice.

"Yes," I repeated for the second time. "Two o'clock. With the editor."

"The editor?" he repeated blankly.

"Yes. A--" Vasily looked at his notebook. "Jordan Small?"

"Jordan?"

Getting a bit exasperated, I tried a different tact. "Is he even in?"

"Who?"

"Jordan."

"*She* is at lunch."

"Okay. When does she return?"

"From what?"

"Lunch," I replied, suddenly thinking I was stuck in the middle of a classic Abbott and Costello skit.

"About one," he said.

"Look, Mike," I said, reading the name from the plate on the desk. "Can we go in?"

"In?"

I pointed to the only other door in the small office that clearly led to an office. The *Journal* appeared to be smaller than I realized.

"Sure," he said. To my surprise, he stood and opened the door for us.

An older woman with short gray hair looked up over her glasses. "Mike?"

"Your two o'clock," he said and toddled back out into the lobby.

"You must be Chief Colbeth," Jordan said as she stood and shook my hand.

"Call me Sean," I smiled. "This is my number two, Vasily Korsokovach."

"Ma'am," he said as we took our seats.

"That's quite a guard dog you have," I said.

"Mike?" Jordan laughed. "He's a bit of an odd duck, but he also can't hear worth squat. He was probably trying to read your lips and failed miserably."

"Good to know," I replied. "Like my staff told you on the phone, we're here regarding the package Ingmar Pelletier sent you."

"Yes," she said as she started shifting the mass of papers on her desk. "It's right... here," she said triumphantly, sliding a Priority Mail package out and handing it to me.

I turned it over and saw it was unopened. "You haven't reviewed it yet?"

"No," she said, spreading her hands over her desk. "Believe it or not, we get hundreds of submissions from researchers across the globe. I'm a little behind getting material out to our peer reviewers for the next issue."

Vasily snorted.

Glaring at him, I asked: "I was under the impression that Ingmar felt like his work would be... prioritized."

"Normally it would," she nodded. "His work on *supernus* has gathered a ton of interest."

I blinked. "Super-what?"

"*Supernus*," she repeated. "It's the new variety he's crafted."

I traded looks with Vasily. "Is it, like, patented or something?"

"Not yet," she replied. "But the new variety has been given conditional approval by the Society."

Slowly, I nodded. "The one running the Symposium that is going on up in Windeport."

"Yes."

I hefted the package. "I need to take this," I said. "Do you want to make copies before I do?"

She raised an eyebrow. "As long as we get it back? No."

I nodded as we stood to go. "I'll make sure we return it to you."

"Great."

"Thank you for your time," I said. "We can see ourselves out."

In the elevator, Vasily asked pointedly, "Are you sure we can return the package to her after we close the investigation?"

"Yes," I said. "There was a reason that Ingmar sent this to her," I replied. "I think once we understand that, we'll feel the same way as he did and want to return it."

Vasily looked skeptical. "Whatever you say, Chief."

Eleven

I left the package and my partner in our hotel room and went to take a walk. Deidre still hadn't returned any of my text messages, and my subsequent calls had gone directly to voicemail. I needed time to think about my next move, and it had been years since I'd wandered the historic streets where the American Revolution was born. Maybe somewhere along the way, inspiration would strike, and I'd figure out what I was going to do.

Without really paying attention, I managed to work my way toward Quincy Market; once the bulk of Faneuil Hall worked its way into my consciousness, I bowed to my inner thirteen-year-old and sought out the soft pretzel vendor my grandfather always took us to when we visited. It was still there on the first floor of the market, and I happily let the wondrous smell wash over me before taking a huge bite of my treasure. Grandfather had been gone for many years now, but as I savored the buttery-salty flavor, and munched more slowly as I worked my way back out and into the Market proper, warm thoughts of summer weekends at his place in Cambridge briefly lifted my spirits.

I found a park bench and sat beneath a leafless maple and watched the late afternoon ebb and flow of pedestrians. A part of me wasn't surprised that Deidre was opting to avoid what she viewed as a possible confrontation. In our decade together, though, I'd generally been the agreeable partner in the relationship, the one to avoid any sort of issues that could lead to uncomfortable moments between us. Save for one, of course: at least, at the time, I'd assumed we were on the same page, but if what Vasily had overhead was accurate, I'd wildly misread my girlfriend when it came to the issue of children.

My ex-girlfriend.

I sighed and took another bite of my pretzel. "Ex-girlfriend," I said aloud, trying to get used to the concept.

After so long with one person, thinking of myself as single was a novelty. I thought I understood why she'd run to Boston, too. In such a big city, she'd easily be able to find a new life and a new me; with the money from the grocery store, she'd have time to land softly, too. It was a solid plan, and one that she had to have been thinking of for a while.

I shook my head as I polished off the last of the pretzel, stood and placed the wax wrapper in a nearby trashcan. Deidre had let me go long before that final night in my bed; looking back now, I could see it had been that fabled goodbye sex -- a passionate reminder for both partners of what had once been.

Torn between not wanting to ambush her and yet wanting some sort of official closure, I decided for the latter and began my trek toward the Boston Harbor Hotel. It wasn't far from Quincy Market, relatively speaking, and I arrived at the recognizable archway just as the long shadows of early evening were inching their way up the side of the towers. I nodded to the doorman and entered the massive tiled foyer, and then paused.

Do I call up to her room? Or hang out in the lobby, hoping for a chance encounter?

The concierge seemed to sense my dithering and wandered over to me, his retail smile pleasant. "Sir? Might I assist?"

I smiled back. "It's a bit awkward," I replied. "My... girlfriend is here for a wedding, and I suddenly had business in Boston and wanted to drop in and surprise her."

"That's romantic!" he said.

"It would be," I agreed. "Except I found out earlier today that she's moving on. And might not actually want to see me. But she doesn't know I know."

The concierge kept smiling. "I see your problem."

"I'm sorry, I'm babbling. I'll just go."

"In a way, maybe I can help," he offered. "Sadly, there is no wedding party here at the moment. There was a party on the prior Friday, and we don't have another until Saturday. It's actually a slow part of the season for us."

I nodded slowly. "I see," I said. "Yes, actually, thank you. That was quite helpful."

"Of course, sir," he smiled and walked back to his station.

I stood for a moment, realizing that Deidre had probably never actually been in Boston. Or if she had, it was on her way to somewhere else. The *where* probably depended on how much she'd gotten from the sale of the grocery store. It started to dawn on me just how significantly I appeared to have hurt her, though again, that last night in the apartment would have argued otherwise. Pulling out my cell phone once more, I tried her number one last time; once more, it went to voicemail, but this time I realized it no longer had her personalized message.

I suspected by the morning, the number would no longer work.

She was truly gone.

I speed dialed Vasily.

"Chief?" he said. "What's up? How did the meet with Deidre go?"

"Absolutely fantastic," I lied.

There was a pause. "That good, eh?"

"Yeah. Listen, did you get a date for your theater outing tonight?"

"Not yet," he said. "You want to come with?" he asked.

"Yes," I said. "Provided we go to a bar first. And I'm not your date, just so we're clear."

"Gotcha," he laughed. "Are you coming back to the Ritz?"

"Yes," I said. "I'll meet you in the lobby."

Twelve

The ringtone of my iPhone burst into my consciousness like a nuclear bomb, causing me to bolt upright in my bed and search for the mushroom cloud. My heart rate slowed slightly when the more logical portion of my brain tamped down the fight-or-flight instincts, though it was a challenge not to smash the phone against the floor to get it to stop. Running one hand through my extremely wild hair, I used the other to unlock the phone. "Chief Colbeth," I said, trying for professional while attempting to ignore the massive headache I appeared to have.

"Sean, what the hell?" came a cheerful voice.

The pounding in my head, however, forced a few extra seconds before comprehension kicked in. "Charlie?" I asked, my mind clearing a bit faster. "What's wrong? Is everything okay?"

"It won't be if you don't get back in time for the party."

"I'm coming back today," I said, still feeling a bit groggy. Sliding out from between the sheets, I padded over to the curtains and pulled one back. A massive beam of sunshine spilled into the room, eliciting a series of curses from the next bed over. Turning, I tried not to smile as Vasily pulled the pillow over his head and continued cursing. "I had an appointment here late yesterday, and it was easier to stay over than get back late."

"I'm a little surprised you haven't started back already. It's not like you to laze around in bed."

My eyes went to the small clock radio on the nightstand, and I tried not to curse myself. It was nearly nine. "I blame Vasily," I said, squinting against the sunshine myself. The throbbing centered between my eyes told me the headache wasn't going away any time soon; I sagged back down on the bed.

"The *Hell* it's my fault," came a muffled response.

"Besides," I continued, "he's really looking forward to the party, too."

"What?!" he hissed as he flipped the pillow off. "I'm not--"

"Good," Charlie was saying as I kept a hand over the receiver to keep her from hearing the continued cursing. "If you can both be here a bit earlier, I could use the help getting the space arranged."

"Will do."

"Your nieces are looking forward to seeing you in costume," she reminded me.

"Are they? I doubt that."

"They are. That was just a pleasant reminder that you'd better not 'forget' to wear it this year."

"Yes, ma'am," I laughed as I hung up and tossed the phone down on the rumpled bedclothes.

Vasily had propped himself up on one arm and was glaring at me. "I had plans tonight."

"No, you didn't," I said. "I know you were going to watch Netflix and hide out in the apartment."

"I *was* going to another party," he said defensively.

"Oh?" I asked, curious despite the pounding in my head. He'd not mentioned anything earlier.

"Yeah," he said.

"When does it start?"

"Sean, I've already committed--"

"I'm sure you did," I replied. "Just like I've committed *us* to help Charlie tonight. What time?"

Groaning, he fell back against the pillow. "I'm not getting out of it, am I?"

"Nope. What time?"

Vasily pulled another pillow over his face. "Ten," came the muffled reply.

"Perfect. We wrap at the Library around seven, so you'll have plenty of time to get to your other party." I waited for a beat. "What are you going as?"

There was a strangled cry under the pillow. "It's so totally *not* appropriate for a kid's party."

I considered my best friend, or what I could see of him beneath the pillow. "I was naive to assume it was a Halloween party, wasn't I?"

He slid the pillow off his face and looked at me sideways. "Partially," he said with a sheepish grin. "Let's just assume it's *not* one you'd ever attend."

I found my eyebrows going up. "In Windeport?" I asked, incredulously.

This time, I got a smirk. "Every town has a dark underbelly." He paused, a wicked gleam to his eyes. "Halloween just provides a mainstream excuse for us to come out from beneath our rocks."

"I don't think I want to know that," I said as I grabbed a change of clothes from my bag and headed for the shower. "Especially since I'm the Chief and all."

The drive back was reasonably uneventful; fortunately, by the time we'd left Boston behind, the hangover had abated, though the sun still threatened to trigger another round of migraines. *Hamilton* had been excellent - somehow, Vasily had scored tickets four rows from the stage - but we'd started and ended the evening in the hotel bar. Deidre's departure from my life had felt like a stray thread I had accidentally pulled, resulting in the unravelling of the whole sweater. Vasily had lent me a compassionate ear as I realized, to my horror, I was finding the thread a lot longer, and a lot more enmeshed in my soul than I would have believed. Drinking had ultimately only made it worse.

No matter how many ways I asked, Vasily steadfastly refused to disclose his costume, but assured me he had figured out a way to make it temporarily kid friendly - provided I allowed him time to stop at the Wal-Mart just outside of town. For my part, I was completely unwilling to tell him what Charlie had cooked up for me and instead redirected the conversation back to the case.

Vasily was at the wheel when we passed through Portland. "I'm still curious as to why Ingmar sent the research to the *Journal*. Was it some sort of revenge, academia style?"

"Maybe," I said. "The whole thing feels a little odd to me."

The envelope was in my briefcase and I pulled it out. The packet was amazingly heavy, and I could feel the hard copy that Barbara Thompson had likely printed for Ingmar. Turning it over, I could see it had been addressed using one of the standard software packages that printed a label from the postal service, with the return address clearly the College of Agriculture.

"God damn," Vasily said. "Open it already."

I laughed and flipped it around again, pulling the tab to sever the seal. Popping open the envelope, I slid out a handsomely bound packet that had a cover letter carefully paperclipped to the top. "There's an intro here," I said, "and it's in longhand."

"Really?"

I scanned the clear strokes on the heavy paper. Ingmar had to have gone through Elementary School when they were still teaching the classic Palmer method, for his writing was exceptionally easy to follow. Mine required constant translation. "It's a personal note," I added before reading it aloud.

Jordan - good to talk to you on the phone. This is the research I told you about. It's imperative you get it out for review as soon as you can - better if you can get it published first.

I feel strongly that a discovery of this nature needs to be shared, freely, with the world. Call me.

Best - Ing.

"Ing?"

"Yeah," I smiled. "Hard to think of him being personable." I looked up at the traffic as we passed the Burger King in Gray. "But more importantly, this indicates he *called* Jordan before he sent the packet."

"She left that out of the conversation, didn't she?"

"Yes," I said. "I think we might have to make a return trip to Boston."

"Great!" Vasily smiled. "I'm up for another show."

I slid the cover letter behind the bound materials, and then peeled back the first page. I quickly found myself lost in the dense scientific text beyond the executive summary that essentially restated what I had heard Menard LaChance espouse at his keynote. I scanned the material lightly, stopping now and then to review a diagram or photo of the research, unsure exactly what it was I had in my hands. As I hit the final summary section of the document, I looked up long enough to see that Vasily had pulled off the Interstate and was just starting the final push cross-country to Windeport.

"Enthralling?" he asked.

"Sorry," I apologized, realizing I'd spent the better part of an hour muttering to myself. "I keep trying to understand what I have here. To be honest, it might as well be ancient Greek."

"I imagine asking Bedard to help is out of the question."

"Pretty much. And we could go to LaChance, but I want someone outside the U to look at it for me."

"What about that visiting professor we had?" Vasily asked. "The guy who was on loan from Orono for a semester?" He laughed slightly. "Speaking of Greek - I think he *was* from Greece, if I remember correctly."

I nodded slowly. "Stellos was his first name, right?"

"Sounds right."

"I'll call Orono when we get to the Station."

I flipped back to the final summary and read it for the third time. LaChance was adamant that the potato he had designed would solve world hunger, essentially, which was a significant statement. If he were right, the value of such a discovery would be worth millions or more to the University - and whoever they licensed it to.

But while that seemed like a lovely motive for murder, LaChance was decidedly *not* dead. The man who helped fund his research *was*. It was a conundrum that was eating away at me.

"I want to look over the finances for the project tomorrow," I said. "I feel like there is something there."

"You've got it, Chief." He looked sidelong at me. "But first, Wal-Mart."

I rolled my eyes.

Thirteen

The *Windeport Not-So-Scary Halloween Party* was something of an institution. I had my own fond memories of heading over to the Windeport Public Library with my mother and joining other kids in wacky games conjured up by librarians fully decked out for the occasion. Charlie had to remind me that *all* the public safety officials had attended year after year, pointedly making the case for my reluctant attendance each October the thirty-first. For as much as I'd enjoyed attending as a child (or teen, for that matter), I'd had no interest in participating as an adult.

And that was *before* she started to insist that we appear in costume.

This particular year, she had carefully waged a charm campaign using her twin daughters against me. For she knew I would do anything for them; and, unfortunately, in a very weak moment, Charlie had them quietly ambush me, begging that I appear as a character from their current favorite cartoon. Unable to refuse the cuteness inherent in eight-year-olds, I agreed without first asking *what* cartoon we were talking about.

As I stared at the black fabric in the bottom of the Amazon box, it only made it marginally better that, according to Charlie's response to my frantic text message, I'd apparently been selected to be a superhero. I looked at my iPhone, hoping to see some sort of Amber Alert or any other global catastrophe. Even a call from the Crime Lab with my results from the bungalow, albeit several days ahead of schedule.

Stubbornly, the iPhone remained silent.

"Vasily!" I hollered.

"Just a sec."

I dumped the box out on the bed and sorted out the contents. I had to admit, Charlie had been surprisingly complete; she'd helpfully texted me a few screencaps of the character in question, and it didn't take long for me to identify the various parts of the costume. There were boots of a sort, a blond wig, a domino mask and two triangular pieces of fabric that apparently went on the wig. A small metallic cylinder with a lighted paw print and a ring box rounded out the supplies.

Vasily knocked at the door, and I turned. Whatever I'd started to say was lost when I saw he was already changed; it took me a moment to take it all in. His hair was out of its requisite ponytail and gently resting on his shoulders, and a long, flowing red cape hung from his shoulders. He was bare chested, but had some sort of odd leather harness that was accentuating his pectorals and six-pack abs. A gladiator-style kilt that matched his cape ran to just above his knees, and leather boots in dark brown finished the look. He had a massive faux stone hammer in one hand.

"Wow," was all I could think to say.

He smiled. "Wal-Mart is truly magical," he said.

"Who *are* you?" I asked.

Vasily rolled his eyes. "You had a sheltered life growing up, Sean. Didn't you read comics at all?"

"No," I admitted. "When I wasn't at the pool, I was doing schoolwork."

"That explains everything," he chuckled. "I am Thor, God of Thunder. And, more recently, a member of the Avengers."

I looked at him. "Uh, *that* Thor looks a bit different..."

"I'm the comic-book version," he smiled, then waited for a beat. "For adults."

My eyes widened in horror. "You can't—"

"The kids won't know," he laughed. "Now, what did you want?"

Tearing my eyes away from my transformed friend, I picked up the one-piece spandex that was the base of the costume. "I don't know what to do with this," I said.

Vasily took the fabric from my hand and then scanned the bed, his eyes widening as he hit on the wig and boots. "Oh... my... *God!*" he cried. "No way!"

"What?" I said, somehow feeling more embarrassed.

"You're going as *Chat Noir!*"

Despite being a decorated, multiple-award-winning, top-notch investigator and the local Chief of Police, I felt my face flame. "I guess," I said. "But this costume! It can't be right. I mean, look at this! I can't wear this!"

Vasily laughed. "That's funny. You nearly paraphrased the character that wears that costume - there's an episode—"

"*Vasily!*"

"Sorry." He shifted the fabric and whistled. "Here's the zipper, it's hidden under this bell here..."

Against my better judgement, in less than twenty minutes, I found myself standing in front of my bathroom mirror encased in what felt like doubly skintight black spandex and a blond wig topped with (what I now knew were) two cat ears. Vasily had just passed in the two boots and I'd been dithering, for I felt ridiculous. Neither the metal tube affixed with Velcro to the small of my back nor the obsidian ring with glowing green paw print helped diffuse my growing anxiety.

"Utterly ridiculous," I said to the image in the mirror.

"We're going to be late," Vasily warned from the other side.

"I still have time." Groaning, I pushed my feet into the boots and zipped them closed; like the costume, the zipper had been hidden behind a seam. Grudgingly, I had to admit that Charlie had gone all out.

"I've got your tail out here," Vasily said.

"My *what?*"

Clearly unable to wait any longer, Vasily pulled open the door and handed me some sort of belt. "Put this on while I dab adhesive on your mask," he said as he took the mask from my hands.

It turned out to be more complicated than it looked, especially with the claw tips in the attached gloves, but I managed to get the belt on as Vasily instructed and found myself with five feet of leather trailing behind me. "Lovely," I groaned. "What kind of superhero has a costume like this?" I said, eyes falling on the stupid golden bell at my throat.

"A very cool one. But you should also know he's just a kid in the show; the costume reflects that."

"Lovely," I breathed, squeezing my eyes shut in the vain hope this was a bad dream.

That proved to be a mistake, for Vasily took that moment to dart in. "Keep those closed for a moment," he instructed as he dabbed something on my lids, then around the orbits of my eyes.

"What are you doing — is that *makeup*?"

"Calm down," he said. He finished and then I felt him place the mask against my face. "Press, firmly, for a few moments while the adhesive sets."

While I stood there, eyes closed, hands to the face, I heard him wash up. "I am going to ban all cameras at this event," I said firmly. "And arrest anyone who defies me."

"I don't think the law is on your side, Chief," he laughed. "Okay, open your eyes."

I blinked my eyes open and saw a completely different person in the mirror. With the mask on, and the eye black he'd put on beneath it, I could nearly convince myself I was that other person I was now seeing in the mirror.

"It's lucky your eyes are green," Vasily laughed. "That happens to be the same as the character, save for the fact they are more cat like, of course."

"Of course," I murmured, turning slightly. The fabric had an odd pattern that caught the light as I shifted my position; suddenly, I was starting to like the idea that I could escape Sean Colbeth for a few hours. "Who am I supposed to be again?"

"Chat Noir. Hero of Paris."

Yes, given everything that had happened over the past twenty-four hours, I could use a few of make-believe. And it *was* in pursuit of a good cause. "C'est fantastique," I said quietly.

"Good," Vasily laughed, "for we are *really* going to be late."

"All right," I said and turned to go. "We'd better walk though. There's no way I'm going to be able to put my wallet or car keys in these pockets."

Fourteen

The moderate weather held, something Vasily truly appreciated given the sparseness of his costume; otherwise, the subzero temps we more often than not experienced on Halloween would have made the five-block walk to the Library rather frigid. Still, the slight ocean breeze seemed to slice right through the thin fabric of my own costume, making the high sixties temp feel brisker than it should have.

Walking seemed to be the order of the day, however. As we approached the grand facade of the Library, I could see the parking lot was full to overflowing with goblins and ghouls of all ages; more were descending from the four corners of the village upon the massive double doors of the main entrance. Those had been flung open wide, with haystacks topped by lit pumpkins setting the mood properly.

Despite my misgivings, the costume seemed to be having the desired effect of bringing back memories of a happier time. We waited for a posse of little ghosts to dash past us before going up the granite steps and entering the magnificent lobby. I only made it three steps into the space before two girls of the same age attacked me from the side. One was dressed as some sort of fox; the other, a turtle. It was hard to tell for sure, though, in the dim lighting.

"Uncle Sean! You came!" they cried in unison, each wrapping a leg in a massive hug.

I leaned down and kept my face impassive but couldn't help arching a masked eyebrow. "I'm sorry, girls - I think you've mistaken me for someone else. I'm Chat Noir."

The younger of Charlie's twins (by a full minute, she would proudly tell you) stepped back, eyes wide. "You *are* Chat Noir!" she squealed with delight. Grabbing her sister by the arm, she tugged her away. "We have to tell mama!" she cried, and the two dashed off into the dark recesses of the building.

"Not bad, Chief," Vasily chuckled. "If you really want to convince them, though, you need to drop in a cat-based pun or two."

Smiling as I stood back up, I pulled up my tail (again). "Seriously? They're eight. And I'm not even good with *normal* puns."

"We learn by doing," he smirked. "I'm going for food," he added as he darted right and left me standing nearly in the center of the lobby solo.

I couldn't help but smile, for Charlie and her staff had outdone themselves once more. The normally grand library had taken on a pleasantly spooky mystique, with cobwebs aplenty and just enough flickering jack-o-lanterns to keep the space lit in a low but agreeable fashion. A small easel was set beside the Circulation Desk, indicating where the various activities were being held; according to the spider-shaped arrow, I deduced that Charlie was likely in the reference stacks in the midst of her famous treasure hunt. Not quite ready to show her the fruits of her efforts, I went in the opposite direction and trailed Vasily toward the food.

All the couches and tables in the main reading room had been shifted to the edges of the space and covered with themed tablecloths. Appropriately gross-looking food was on offer, ranging from Witch's Eyeballs (peeled grapes) to Spiderweb Souffle (cotton-candy covered white cake). A small table at the far end had a stereo turned up high, blasting *Monster Mash* and other favorites; amazing me further, the space was jam-packed with people I'd known since I'd been a little boy.

Every last person was wearing a costume nearly as outrageous as mine - and as a consequence, not one had batted so much as a fake eyelash at the fact that the Chief of Police was wandering among them as a nearly six-foot feline-themed superhero. The doldrums finally chased away, I felt a genuine smile appear as I twirled my tail in one hand and made for the bubbling punch bowl and picked up a skull-shaped mug.

Turning back around, I sipped what turned out to be classic orange Kool-Aid spiked with Sprite and wondered where Charlie would place me this year. The finale every season was a trick or treat trail that covered nearly every square inch of the library - our more friendly version of the Haunted House. In years past, I'd been stationed at the exit in my usual Windeport PD uniform, solemnly imploring the departing goblins to "be safe," but I suspected strongly Charlie had a much different plan in mind now that I was in costume. I was in the middle of rolling my eyes at the thought when I felt someone yanking at my tail.

"Seriously, Vasily," I groaned as I turned. "Aren't you just a little old--" I started before choking back the rest of my admonition, masked eyes widening as they saw it was a tall woman who had my tail in one hand.

A tall, amazingly *beautiful* woman, herself wearing an extremely form-fitting red-with-black polka-dotted costume and matching domino mask. As strange as the metallic baton at my back was, *she* appeared to be wearing a yo-yo on her hip. I knew my eyes had travelled up and down her form before I'd had the presence of mind to lock them on her face in a more professional manner as befitting the Chief of Police. "Uh, hi..."

"Hey, kitty," she said. "Purrfect evening, isn't it?" she asked as she dropped my tail to the floor.

"It is," I smiled back. "I'm Chat Noir," I said foolishly, wondering where my sanity had run off to.

"I know," she laughed. "I'm Ladybug."

"Are you?" I said, blinking. "I feel like I'm missing something here."

"You are," she winked. "I'm Suzanne," she laughed as she held out a gloved hand.

"Sean," I said, taking her hand. "A pleasure. So, what am I missing?"

"Your nieces will probably tell you," she smiled, "but you should probably know that the character you're supposed to be is wildly in love with my character."

Beginning to see Charlie's hand in this, I asked: "Indeed. Is it reciprocal?"

"Not exactly," she explained as we moved away from the crowd and toward the lobby. "As a matter of fact, the alter-ego for Ladybug is madly in love with the alter-ego of Chat."

I found my head spinning slightly. "This is a cartoon, right? For kids?"

"So they tell me."

We found a quiet nook by the Circulation Desk. "You must be new in town," I said, trying for a casual conversation despite standing there in black spandex. "I don't recall seeing you here last year."

"I arrived last week," she nodded. "I'm taking over Doctor Philbert's practice."

My masked eyes widened. I had heard the rumors that someone from away - i.e. out of state - would be replacing our retiring general practitioner. "Concord, right?"

"No, I'm originally from Ellsworth. But I spent the last ten years at a practice in North Conway."

"Ah. I knew it was a 'c' city. Why leave the Granite State for the coast?"

"I was looking for a change," she smiled, but there was a tenseness to it, and she looked down at her own boots. There was a story there that she wasn't ready to tell. Instead, she added, "I heard that Windeport was a quaint, quiet little village in need of a doctor." She looked at me again directly, and I saw she had the purest blue eyes I'd ever seen. "Then you go and have a murder less than ten days into my stay," she laughed.

"It's not a common occurrence," I assured her.

"I'm sure you tell all the bugs that," she smiled, brushing back a stray lock of raven black hair.

"That's quite a wig," I said suddenly. "I don't know about you, but mine is itching like crazy."

Suzanne laughed. "Mine's not a wig," she chuckled. "But those ears of yours are *cute*."

Flushing slightly, I thought of a change of subject. "Are you keeping the house?" I asked.

"Where the practice is now? No," she said. "He's sold it so he can move to Florida. I'm actually leasing space in one of the old brick blocks along Route One. I guess it used to have a pharmacy in it? Maybe you know the one?"

"I do," I replied. "Since it was my family that used to run it."

"Really?" she asked. "Charlie said you were a police officer. Not a pharmacist?"

"Hence why the space was available," I laughed. "But I admit I'll miss the soda fountain." *And my apartment,* I added mentally.

"I can keep it if it helps," she said, and it caught me that she was serious.

"Nah. Everything changes with time." I picked my tail up. "For instance, a week ago, I wouldn't have been caught dead in an outfit like this."

"Really? What changed?"

"It's a long story but suffice to say I blame a super potato."

"Are you talking about *supernus*?" Suzanne asked unexpectedly.

I felt the surprise on my face. "Yes," I said. "How did you hear about it?" I asked, arching a masked eyebrow.

"I was a bio major," she said patiently. "It's kind of a prerequisite for being a doctor. My bachelor's degree is from the University; I had Doctor Pelletier for BIO-100."

"Didn't we all," I replied. "I wonder, Doctor, if you'd be willing to consult on something…?"

Fifteen

Snagging a second skull cup of punch for Suzanne, I gently wove us through the crowd and managed to escape the library before Charlie noticed our absence. The Public Safety building was just a half block further down the street, and it was still reasonably warm. But a few moments into our sojourn, I could tell Suzanne's costume was as thin as my own when she tried to suppress a shiver brought on by the ongoing ocean breeze. "This could wait until the morning," I said, pausing on the sidewalk with a gloved hand on her shoulder.

"No, I've got a full schedule tomorrow," she smiled. "Besides, you've piqued my curiosity."

"All right," I smiled, and we continued.

We found poor Caitlyn behind the desk, having drawn the unlucky short straw to be on the phones for the evening; she was taking it with her usual aplomb, and was rocking a rather amazing costume. "Hermione Granger, right?" I said as we stepped to the desk.

"Chief…?" Caitlyn said, eyes wide as she took in my outfit, cat ears to boots. "You're… Chat Noir?"

I sighed. "I have to be the only person on the face of this planet who doesn't know about this show," I said, turning to Suzanne.

"Yes," she replied with a sweet grin.

"Maybe you can give me a curated set of episodes, then," I laughed. "I fear this won't be the last time Charlie makes me use this costume."

"And they say you're not an investigator," Suzanne chuckled. "I'd be happy to."

"Good." Something in my heart clicked, the tiny portion that had apparently been frozen somewhere in the arctic, but I set it aside for the moment. I turned back to Caitlyn and arched one of those masked eyebrows. "As you can imagine, I don't have my ID with me…"

"I can't possibly break protocol, Chief," Caitlyn said and for a long, long moment I thought she was going to deny me access to my office. But then she broke into a wide grin and depressed the hidden button beneath the reception desk, unlatching the door to the back.

"Hermione to the fullest," I said, narrowing my eyes at her.

"If you have a role to play," she laughed. "Play it well."

"I'll keep that in mind during your next Performance Appraisal," I warned good naturedly. "C'mon, Ladybug, let's get to the Cat Cave."

"Nice thought, but wrong comic," Suzanne said as she followed me through and down the short hallway to the bullpen.

I paused at the intersection. "He's got to have a secret lair. They *all* have one."

"Well, not this once. For the bulk of the series, he's a teenager living at home."

I threw my claw-tipped hands into the air and continued toward my office. "I appear to have a lot to learn," I muttered as I snapped on the light over the desk and slid around to grab the file from the *Journal*. It took two tries to sit down without snagging my tail; I didn't quite dare to remove the baton-thing and wound up sitting on the edge of my chair.

Suzanne appeared to take my struggles in stride. For her part, she gracefully settled into one of the two mid-century behemoth visitor chairs before leaning forward to take the file. "This is what Ingmar Pelletier apparently sent to the *American Journal of Potato Research* for immediate peer review and subsequent publication."

She pulled the sheaf of paper out and her masked eyes popped wide. "Good Lord. This is the entire project file, isn't it?"

"Yes," I nodded, absently sitting back before gouging the baton into my back. Smothering a curse, I continued. "I gathered he did it against the standard protocol for the University. And based on what I could understand of what I was reading — I'm not a scientist, obviously — it seemed like he sent both the baby *and* the bathtub."

"He did," she whistled as she squinted at the paper. Sheepishly, she looked up. "Middle-age sucks," she said. "You don't happen to have cheaters, do you?"

That funny feeling appeared in my heart again. "I might," I said, as I pulled open a drawer and retrieved three sets of standard issue pharmacy glasses. Carefully sliding them to her, I added in a conspiratorial tone of voice: "As far as my staff knows, I still have perfect 20/20 vision."

She slowly nodded. "Contacts?" she said as she selected a particular power - plus one, same as me I noted.

"Yes." I watched as she held them up to her mask and started reading the page anew. It was such an odd visual and yet, given how the day had been going, seemed perfectly in line with life at the moment. "Don't worry, madam. Your secret is safe with me."

Suzanne looked over the half-moon lenses, those blues eyes sparkling with some sort of mischief I could only guess at. "It's 'Milady,' if you want to stay in character."

"Of course, Milady," I intoned, causing her to burst into laughter, a rich sound that filled my office from end to end. It was infectious enough I found myself smiling. "Can I offer you coffee? I don't usually have anything this late, but I've been known to make exceptions."

"God, yes, please," she said. "We learn early in Med School to mainline caffeine, and I'm down a few grams."

I stood and managed not to kill myself by tripping over the tail and moved to my personal Keurig.

"This is absolutely insane," Suzanne said as she flipped the pages, absorbing what she was reading far more rapidly than I had. "I am a little rusty around the edges for some of the more esoteric formulae, but if I am reading this tech note correctly, these potatoes have the equivalent of a white blood cell..."

Popping a pod into the Keurig, I nodded, managing to jingle the damn bell in the process. It tinkled cheerily as the coffee brewed. "That was part of the keynote last night. It sounded unreal - like a bad science fiction movie."

"You're not far off," she murmured.

We lapsed into a pleasant silence, filled only by the occasional rustle as she shifted pages and the sputtering of the Keurig. "How do you like your coffee?"

"Black, straight up," she said.

I carried two mugs over to my massive desk and opted to lean against the front beside her. It was far more comfortable than sitting, though for some reason, I suddenly had the urge to perch atop the blotter, cat-like. I needed to get out of that costume.

Sipping my coffee, I patiently waited. At one point, Suzanne asked for some paper and started to scribble notes as she read; flipping back and forth, she kept jotting notes. I wasn't sure, but the further she got into the document, the more excitedly she wrote on the legal pad.

Finally, two cups of coffee and about ninety minutes later, she tossed everything back on my desk and swiveled so she could lean her back against one arm of the chair and drape her legs over the other. Even with the mask hiding most of her beautiful face, I could see she was wearing a deeply thoughtful expression.

"Does it do what LaChance claims?" I ventured, sipping on my third cup of coffee, and knowing I wasn't going to be getting any sleep as a result.

Idly, she snapped the yo-yo from her waist and started twirling it over the edge of the chair. "No," she said after a long moment. "But you'd be better served having a real botanist look this over, not a mass-spectrum biology major."

"I have a contact up in Orono - if he's still alive, that is." I leaned forward, the bell tinkling slightly as I did so. "What did you see?"

"This paper is expertly done," she said slowly. "There is enough data presented to make a prima facie case that *supernus* is possible. In fact, they did appear to have successfully grown at least three root crops in the second phase of the experiment."

She slid out of her chair and flipped through her notes. "The third phase would have involved the extension, and there is a superficial set of data validating the second phase results."

I nodded. "If I'm following, the in-lab experiment was successful?"

"Yes."

"And the extended test with farmers outside the University was a failure?"

"Not exactly," she said. "Data is included from a test with a local farmer, but the trial was pretty small - not much larger than if they'd grown it inside a greenhouse at the University." She looked back at me. "The supporting data from the other farmers - there are always more farmers than one in these tests - that data is missing." Suzanne leaned back again. "And there should have been a much, much larger test."

Grabbing her mug, she drew in another mouthful of coffee. "What data they have, though, glosses over the fact that the potatoes didn't yield more than a five percent rate - and that was in a controlled environment. I suspect if actual in-field planting had taken place, all the crops failed. Spectacularly."

"Huh," I said. "This definitely changes my view of why Ingmar sent the packet."

"It does?"

"Yeah." I sipped again. "Just based on what we know so far, it felt like he'd sent the info for wider publication to prevent the University from selling the discovery to the highest bidder."

"That would be a noble reason," she nodded.

"Yeah. But not one that I can draw a motive for murder out of. Sure, he'd piss off a lot of people, but in the end, the University was still in line to recoup their expenses and profit somewhat on the patent."

She nodded again. "But this isn't a viable project," she pointed out. "I only have an undergraduate degree in the field; any Ph.D. worth their salt would see through this if it had gone through the peer review process."

"Right - exactly. I think he sent it to the *Journal* to blow the cover off this project." I paused, then added, "And *that* is a valid motive for murder."

Sixteen

I thought we'd managed to sneak back into the Library without drawing attention to our absence, but that fantasy dissolved when my twin nieces pounced on me once more in the lobby. "Chat! Where have you *been*?" the turtle-wearing one practically screamed.

Thinking fast, I shot a look at Suzanne. "Ladybug and I had to go fight a, uh…"

"Akuma," she helpfully provided, then leaned down. "I'm sorry we didn't call on you, Carapace, but it was an overgrown… vegetable… and took multiple Lucky Charms to take out. We didn't have time to call for reinforcements."

"Right," I nodded as if I had any idea what she'd just said.

"Wow! *Really*! You've got to tell mama!" she cried out and started tugging both of us toward the stacks.

As we were being dragged toward Charlie and certain doom, I turned to Suzanne. "Carapace? Akuma? What is this language?" I waited a beat, then asked, "And why did you come as Ladybug, anyway?"

Suzanne flushed slightly as we ducked around the guests and headed toward the far corner of the reference area. Charlie had set up shop with a massive cauldron full of candy and was doling out healthy doses to her gleeful patrons. "I won't lie," she said quietly. "Charlie told me you were coming as Chat Noir a few days ago. I just assumed you were a fan of the show, like I am. I thought it would be fun to hang with a fellow Miraculer."

I detached myself from my minder who ran ahead to her mother, and put a hand on Suzanne's shoulder, unsure of why I felt I needed to convince her. I wondered if I was overcompensating for having parted ways with my girlfriend less than a day earlier. Whether from the costume, or the general atmosphere of the party, my normal barriers were down, and I was unable to stop from leaning toward her ear and softly whispering: "I am *most definitely* a fan, Milady. I just didn't know it until today."

She smiled at me and nodded. "Good," she replied. "I think I'm going to like it here in Windeport."

"Yes," I agreed. "And now that you know who the top Chat is around here..."

Suzanne groaned. "You were doing so well, too."

"Sorry," I said sheepishly. "This is all new to me. Anyway... how do you know Charlie?"

"The Library," she said. "Even in the age of the internet, it's still the best place in any town to get information. She put me in touch with the real estate agent I'm using and - this is embarrassing actually," she demurred.

My masked eyes widened, and I leaned closer, trying to ignore how perfectly the floral perfume she was wearing complimented her outfit. "You can tell me," I whispered.

Blushing slightly, she shifted on her feet. "Well... she found out I'd tried to book a room up at the Colonial until my apartment is ready. She told me flatly that it wasn't worth the money and insisted I stay with her and the kids."

"That sounds like Charlie," I smiled, though my stomach twisted slightly at the realization I was likely in the very apartment she was waiting to get into. Further conversation stalled out as a shadow crossed her face. I turned and a wildly smiling Charlie was there, towering over us. "Jesus, cousin," I said, stepping back. "You were already six feet tall! You didn't need the lifts!"

Wrapping me in a big hug, she laughed. "It's my only chance to be taller than you, Sean."

I rolled my eyes. "Whatever," I smiled.

"I see you've met my new roomie," Charlie said as she released me and hugged Suzanne. "God, you two look adorable," she gushed as she stepped back and retrieved her iPhone.

I held up a gloved hand. "Now wait just a damn minute—"

"Too late," she cackled. "This is now immortalized on our Facebook page."

"Lovely," I groaned, lowering my hand.

As Charlie slipped her phone back into a pocket, I took stock of her outfit. Her hair was died three shades of something that was hard to pick up in the murky light of the party and was sporting a unicorn horn that was sprouting from a headband. A massively oversized white sweater had a rainbow wrapped around the middle, and as she turned, sequins picked up the light. Multiple pillows or some sort of fill material had given her a rather rotund torso, completely masking the fact that she was nearly rail thin. White tights and white boots with massive platforms finished the deal.

Charlie caught the question on my lips. "Unicorn, or as close as I could get at the last minute. The kids were supposed to be Tweedle Dee and Tweedle Dum until they found out their favorite uncle was coming as Chat Noir." She tried to stifle a yawn. "I was up until two finishing their costumes."

I widened my masked eyes. "Wait... but it was in an Amazon box..."

Charlie smiled and took a small bow. "I see the Great Detective is just now realizing why I took all of those measurements last spring."

"You *said* you were knitting me a sweater," I replied defensively. "Not making me a spandex onesie... though it was odd you needed my inseam." I looked to Suzanne. "I suppose she made yours, too?"

"Heavens no," Suzanne laughed. "I got mine from a cosplay store on the internet last year so I could wear it to Comic-Con." She looked off to the side and then smiled again. "I'm off to the little bug's room. Will you be here when I get back?"

I looked to Charlie. "I don't think my term is up yet, no."

"Good," she laughed again and disappeared into the crowd.

I narrowed my masked eyes at my cousin. "Seriously?"

Charlie kept smiling and moved us to a quieter corner of the room. "She's a keeper."

"Charlie, I don't know what you're about—"

"Sean, you're an idiot. At least when it comes to relationships."

My masked eyes narrowed a bit. "Don't mince words, Cousin. Tell me what you really think."

"All right," she replied, taking me literally. "The entire village knew Deidre was leaving town months ago. You can't have been oblivious enough to have not realized she was spending more time away than here."

I stared at Charlie.

"I stand corrected." Her eyes took on a bit of concern mixed with a tinge of disgust - but not necessarily directed at me. "It's not entirely your fault, but you do bury yourself in your work. At least, since your mother passed away. Deidre told anyone who would listen that she'd taken a backseat to you travelling the state and consulting."

My eyes narrowed further. "She never said that to me. Never gave me the slightest hint."

"You've been with her ten years, Sean. You knew her better than us - would she have confronted you? Or would she have tried to change your mind more subtly?"

I nodded slowly. "She wasn't into confrontation," I admitted. "Neither am I, especially." Idly, I picked up my tail and started to twirl it. "I thought we communicated better than most. I can't believe she didn't at least try to talk to me."

"I'm sure she did, and you just didn't realize it. So instead, she talks to the baker. To her hairdresser. To me, for Christ's sake."

My head snapped to hers. "Charlie - you could've said something!"

"Not my place," she said. "But you will recall multiple attempts to get the two of you over, together, for dinner. At holidays or for no reason at all."

I nodded slowly. "Something always came up."

"For you. Or her." Charlie put a hand to my shoulder. "To be honest,

I'm surprised it lasted this long. You weren't a good match." She paused again. "You have to know that, in your heart of heart. I mean, come on! You go all the way to Boston, find out she's left, and then *come home.* Any broken-hearted lover worth their salt would have hurried after their soulmate to try and win them back."

I thought about that for a moment. Charlie was right, the hole that *should* be in my heart wasn't there; Deidre *had* left me a long time ago. My eyes snapped back to hers, though. "How did you know I was following up her story?" I asked pointedly. "Even *I* didn't know what I was going to do until the day before yesterday."

Charlie laughed. "Who do you think created Vasily's costume?" she chuckled. "That number two of yours was as concerned as the rest of us. In fact, if you ask him, I think he'll tell you what he found out about Deidre."

My eyes widened. "Found out?"

Charlie lowered her voice more. "When word spread that the IGA was on the market, he started to do some digging and then paid close attention to Deidre's movements. He wasn't entirely comfortable coming to you with what he found, though, for he felt like you might assume he had ulterior motives."

"Then he doesn't know me very well," I said tightly.

"Oh, he knows you better than you think, Sean," she said softly. "So, he came to me."

"What did he find?"

"Not my story to tell," she said. "But I suspect after tonight, you'll be ready to hear it."

"What the hell? Does the entire village know? Everything?"

"Not everything. But most everything."

"Jesus."

"No need to involve him," Charlie said sweetly.

My eyes scanned the room and saw Suzanne laughing with the twins; she turned and smiled in my direction. Despite my anger with my cousin, I found myself returning the smile. "Damn you," I breathed.

"You can thank me later," she said. "Suzanne is nothing like Deidre, though. Consider yourself warned."

"The jury is still out on that," I said, then added grudgingly, "but the prosecution has made a good case." I sighed. "Fortunately, Ladybug over there was helpful translating some of Menard LaChance's research for me."

"I heard about Ingmar," Charlie replied. "Terrible. A nicer man you'd not find anywhere; I can't believe anyone would want to kill him."

"If what Suzanne told me is accurate, I might be getting a clearer picture of that."

Charlie clucked. "Poor soul. Heard he was selling the house to avoid foreclosure, too."

I felt my masked eyes widen. "Sorry?"

"You didn't know? He had a double mortgage on that beautiful house. Been in the family since the late forties. Elaine is worried that she's going to have to take it on the chin as a short sale."

"But he drove an ancient truck," I said, puzzled. "And his house is practically empty of furniture - where did he spend the money?"

"That's a good question," Charlie said sweetly. "Too bad we don't have a detective on the case."

"Careful, Cousin," I said slyly as I held up the gloved hand that had the glowing paw-print ring. "I might just Catastrophe my way through this Library of yours, with talk like that."

Charlie started laughing so hard, tears began streaming down her face. In between great gasps, she managed to get out, "Cataclysm... hoo! It's... Cataclysm!"

"Well whatever," I tried to say hotly, but her laughter was so infectious, found myself smiling.

Suzanne returned at that point, took in the scene, and then turned an arched eyebrow on me.

"It's not my fault," I said with a grand smile.

"Right," she laughed.

Charlie kept laughing as she turned and wandered back toward the cauldron and her waiting fans, wiping away the tears as she went. I watched her navigate the thinning crowd as if she weren't wearing those massive lifts and wondered if I'd ever be capable of not tripping over my tail. I twirled it thoughtfully and turned back to Suzanne.

Maybe it was the night, or the insanity of standing there in a feline-themed superhero costume. Or maybe, simply, it was the part of me that had decided to move on. Was it possible? Was I leaping from one fire to another? I looked down at the leather belt in my hand and knew I wasn't the same man I'd been just a few days earlier. Maybe I hadn't been for some time. This murder had changed things, and I thought perhaps I'd only begun to see the truth beneath the lies I'd been living with.

Maybe I was ready to change the story. Finally.

I paused for a long moment, wondering if I really wanted to follow the thread I was pulling. The rational part of my brain was screaming *full stop*; if I kept going, I ran the real risk of screwing up another relationship before it had practically begun. But the ache was there now, almost as if I had been anesthetized and was just beginning to feel the pain of losing Deidre, bringing with it a nearly visceral need to make it go away.

Looking at Suzanne's eyes, I could see a cautious interest there. Somehow, without asking about it, I knew she'd been hurt, too. That voice in my head was screaming louder and for one of the few times in my adult life, I suddenly was wracked with indecision.

"Sean?" Suzanne asked, eyes now full of concern and worry. "You look lost at sea. What's wrong?"

Rational won out, but it was a tight race.

I crafted a smile close to what I had seen in one of the screenshots Charlie had sent over. "It's been a long day, and I think I'm more tired than I realized. I was about to ask you to sneak away with me to watch the moon rise over the ocean and the stars as they move across the sky - I know an exceptional rooftop with an insane view - but I'm probably not good company. And..." I trailed off.

Suzanne smiled warmly. "And, what?" she prompted, her eyes dancing merrily in the light.

I decided it best not to tell her what I was genuinely thinking - especially given how form-fitting my costume was. I found myself silently thankful for the low lighting. "And... you barely know me. I don't want you to think I'm... Damn. How do I say this without sounding like an idiot?" I asked.

She nodded and ran her hand down my costumed bicep, the smile growing wider. "I understand completely. How about this? Want to meet for coffee tomorrow at that cute little bakery just off Main Street? I don't have to get to the practice until eight - so, say, seven?"

"Sure," I replied, then smiled a bit more slyly. Arching a masked eyebrow, I asked: "Do I need to wear my costume? You might not recognize my civilian alter-ego."

Suzanne leaned up to an ear. "I think I can find the kitty beneath the mask tomorrow," she whispered quietly.

I bowed grandly - just as the character had in one of the other photos Charlie had given me. "Then until the morrow, Milady."

Seventeen

Wanting to make sure I was at Calista's Bakery on time, I skipped the weight training portion of practice the following morning and went from the pool straight to the SUV. As was typical for Maine, the first of November had dawned chilly, completely erasing any memories of the warmer Halloween evening we'd been blessed with. As I slid into the driver's seat of the SUV, the icy coldness of the pleather shot right through the thin material of my warmups, reminding me that all things change - especially seasons.

Calista's Bakery was another longtime institution in Windeport, having sat on the corner of Route One and Maple Street since the turn of the prior century. The brick building stood back from the street and was, remarkably, unaltered from its original construction save for the inevitable nods to modernization: power and telephone lines had been run to the rear and attached via a tasteful filigreed pipe that matched appointments around the windows and door, marking it as a true French bakery.

Seven was the middle of rush hour, at least as far as it went in Windeport. I pulled into the second to last spot of the small parking lot and recognized vehicles belonging to Charlie, Caitlyn, Sylvia and the current chair of the Village Council, Doug Hansen. Passing through the outer half-height wrought iron gate that rimmed the outdoor cafe, I held the door open for Sylvia to bustle out with a mouthful of pastry, hot coffee, and a nod of appreciation. Smiling, I stepped into the pleasantly warm shop and was unsurprised to find it full to overflowing.

As I scanned the crowd for Suzanne, I could smell fresh blueberry muffins were on offer that morning, commingled with the special grind of coffee the current Calista had created a few years back. I'd long since forgotten how many generations Barb was removed from the founder of the bakery; I could see her behind the counter, dressed in her flour-stained apron and looking for all the world as though she were in her personal version of heaven as she wrapped some goodies for a customer. Every time I saw her — and the pure joy she had for baking and the happiness it provided her clientele – it reminded me that people *can* land in their dream jobs. Barb had been miserable as a CPA down in Portland and only realized what her passion was upon her originally temporary return when her mother had taken ill.

That was more than eight years ago now; Cindy had recovered fully and was still back in the kitchen, churning out cakes and pies and bread and just about anything you could think of. Barb had taken on more of the business end of things, but other than that, it was sometimes hard to tell which one of them had more fun.

"Sean!" I heard and turned to see Suzanne had beaten me to the punch. She waved to me from a small two-top nestled into one of the two leaded-glass bow windows that made up the bulk of the street-facing wall.

I nodded to the people I knew as I made my way through the crowded array of tables and patrons and slid into a small chair. "Good morning, Princess," I said.

Suzanne arched an eyebrow. "Princess?"

I smiled as I waved to the overburdened waitress working the cafe tables. "I may or may not have watched a few episodes before falling asleep last night."

"I see," she smiled wider. "But Chat only uses that nickname for Marinette."

"Oops. My cover is blown," I laughed as Linda arrived.

"Chief," she nodded, her hair tumbling out of her bun in more places than I could count. "The usual?"

"Yes," I said. "And whatever my..." I paused, grinning evilly, "lady... friend here would like."

Linda turned to Suzanne. "Coffee, black, and spinach quiche."

"Got it," Linda said and whisked away. Less than a blink of an eye later, two mugs appeared along with a steaming carafe of coffee.

Pouring the black gold into our mugs, I looked to Suzanne. "You were incredibly helpful last night," I said. "If I didn't thank you enough last night, I just want to be on the record fully now."

Cupping her mug, handle toward me, she nodded. "My pleasure. I don't get to trot out the Biology degree often these days. At least, not the botany part."

"I assumed those were two different disciplines," I said as I sipped my coffee. I tried not to moan too loudly.

"It's a holy war to be sure," she laughed. "Let's just say they are related sciences and leave it at that."

"Safe decision, I think."

"Yeah." She sipped her coffee again. "Not that I was spying last night, but what was that medal you had on the wall?"

"In my office?"

"Yeah. The one with the photo - it looked like something swimming related."

"And a product of its era, too," I laughed. "I don't miss those full body swimsuits."

Her eyes widened. "Oh. My. God," she said, recognition dawning in her eyes. "You're *that* Sean Colbeth?"

I couldn't help but smile. It had been years since anyone recognized me from my time at the Olympics. "In the flesh."

"That... that was the four-hundred butterfly? The race you won by, like, point-zero-two? The *gold* medal?"

"Yep," I said, suddenly flushing and hiding it slightly by taking another sip.

"Holy mother of God," she breathed. "What was it like?"

"Athens?" I replied and sat back a bit in the small chair. "You know, it's kind of a blur now. I was just barely eighteen when the games started, first semester freshmen here at the University. We flew in a few days early but stayed in our own little compound; they bussed us to the pool - which was insanely hot in that sun, by the way - and then made sure that we were rounded up and back at the dorms for dinner and bed."

"You must have seen some of the city, though," she said.

"Not really. I saw more of Beijing in '08, but I had more time, then too." I smiled. "Vasily was on the team with me and he was far more willing to break protocol and escape into the city after we were done for the day."

"You made the team *twice*?"

"Yeah. I was only on the relays in Beijing, though; my day had passed. I did get us to the final and in the center lanes, so there's that."

"That... that was a gold medal team, too!"

"It was," I said, smiling slightly, "but that medal stays in my safety deposit box at the bank."

Suzanne started to say something but held off as Linda re-appeared with her quiche and my bowl of oatmeal. She arched an eyebrow as I spooned some of the fresh berries from the smaller side bowl and mixed it together. "Oatmeal? In a bakery?"

"Barb has a farmer in Vermont that she buys the oats from," I explained. "She uses it in her baking, but also makes her own take on oatmeal. Best in the state, and," I said leaning in conspiratorially, "I still watch my figure."

"That was quite obvious last night, kitty," she said with a devilish smile.

I could feel my face flaming a bit - even in my mid-thirties, I could still get embarrassed when women noticed my physical assets. "Uh, thanks," I said. "I've never been able to quit the habit," I added, waving to the team sweatshirt I was wearing.

"Every day?"

"All but Sunday." I tucked into my steaming oatmeal.

Suzanne took a forkful of quiche and closed her eyes in bliss. "This was the first dish I tried when I got back, and I've had it nearly every morning since. I don't know what she puts into it, but I'd eat a whole one if I could get my hands on it."

"I feel the same about the sourdough baguettes," I confessed.

We ate in companionable silence for a bit, and then Suzanne looked up from her half-eaten plate. "I don't want to pry," she said carefully, "but Charlie told me a little bit about what happened to you."

I spooned up a random blueberry. "Yeah," I replied. "The only one not in on the secret was me, apparently," I laughed mirthlessly. "But at the end of the day, I probably gave Deidre plenty of reasons to leave."

"Why would you think that?"

I sighed, and partially wondered why I felt comfortable discussing any of this with Suzanne. "My mother passed away about two years ago," I said. "We were close - not unable-to-cut-the-apron-string close, mind you, but I saw her most days and had dinner with her and Father every Sunday. They lived in a bungalow not far from where Ingmar lived, actually; Father sold it and the pharmacy business to move to Florida." I paused and added a bit absently, "Now he's sold the building too. I've got to be out of the apartment by the fifteenth."

Suzanne's eyes widened. "I didn't realize you were the tenant," she said. "I'm sorry to displace you! I can find—"

"No," I said firmly. "It's time for a change. I have my eye on something." I scooped the final bit of oatmeal from the bottom of the bowl. "Much like my father, I initially had a hard time with Mom's passing. I know I threw myself into work, and it became a pattern I couldn't break out of." I looked at her deep blue eyes. "If nothing else, Deidre's method of exiting our relationship underscored just how blind I'd become – to life outside of my career or the pool." I looked away for a moment. "To her."

"Sean, that's nuts. Everyone goes through grief differently," she said. "Trust me, I'm—"

"A doctor?" I added with a laugh.

"Exactly," she smiled. "I've dealt with plenty of patients and family members who've had difficult losses, for a variety of reasons. There's no simple answer."

I sipped my coffee and didn't realize I'd been so engrossed in our conversation that I'd missed Linda refilling it. "I wouldn't presume to dispute you—"

"That is wise," she smiled.

I laughed. "Anyway, until a few days ago, I didn't realize it was over. I had been ducking the truth. Lying to myself that everything was fine. That this was my new normal." I laughed again; even to my own ears, it was a bit darker. "All the while, my girlfriend is selling her business and removing her stuff from our apartment. And lying about what she's doing in Boston."

"Acceptance is the first step," she said softly. "Not just in grief."

"Yeah," I said. "I've only just realized that." I smiled. "Do I also hear the hint of personal experience in that wisdom?"

Suzanne dropped her gaze to her now empty plate and pivoted her fork on one tine. "Perhaps?" she answered.

She'd tried to mask it, but I'd seen the pain in those deep blue eyes of hers. Pain that mirrored my own. "Well," I said slowly as I drained the last of my coffee. "When you feel up to sharing some pointers, I think I'm in a receptive state."

Suzanne looked up and smiled. "Really?"

"Yeah, I think I might be," I replied with a wry smile. Taking a deep breath, I plowed forward. "Look… I don't want you to think this is some freaky rebound thing, but… I would like to get to know you. Better. So, when you are ready, I'm here to listen."

She considered me for a moment. "You are a good listener, I'll wager."

"Occupational hazard," I shrugged, and then looked at my iPhone. "I've got to get going," I said as I waved to Linda for the check. "What time are you done today?"

"Last patient is around five," she said. "Another hour of paperwork, so, maybe six. Why?"

"My Aunt runs Millie's on the Wharf," I said as I paid the tab. "As it happens, I have a standing reservation on Thursdays."

"I'd like that," she said. "I had the haddock last week and it was wonderful."

"Good. I'm there at six thirty." I stood and smiled. "I'll warn you, though. I never know who Vasily will bring as a date."

Suzanne smiled wider. "I can imagine."

Eighteen

Vasily was waiting in my office when I breezed in a few minutes past eight. I'd intended to catch a shower in the small locker room we had at the station and change into my standard attire, but he was fairly vibrating with excitement when he turned at my entrance. "Chief," he smiled.

I dropped my duffel bag into the second visitor chair and redirected to my personal Keurig for my fourth cup of the morning. "Something interesting came across your desk this morning, I take it," I said as I waited for the machine to warm up.

"Crime lab report came back last night, along with the final report from Heather."

"Did you get any sleep last night?" I asked, smiling. While I'd not heard him return from his more adult Halloween party, I *had* caught the quiet footsteps of his date tiptoeing back out of the apartment before we left for the pool.

Vasily smiled. "Not really," he laughed, "but it's a pleasant tired."

I took the mug and watched the steam as it wafted off the surface of the liquid, then turned to lean against the counter. "All right."

"Bullet is definitely from a Glock, but that is about all they can tell us. The grooves suggest it might be a 17, 18, 19 or 26 but it's not conclusive." He looked up from the report on his tablet. "I'd bet on the 17, since it's a popular model for those who favor concealed-carry."

"You're presuming whoever shot Ingmar was trying to hide in plain sight."

"It seems logical, given the fact it took place in the exposed carport."

I nodded. "I suppose it is. So, we already *knew* he was shot; you're telling me it was -- maybe -- a Glock? And that the person who used it - if they owned it, which is a stretch - likely had a concealed-carry?"

"I agree it's thin," Vasily said, and I could see I'd deflated him slightly.

"It's *something*," I corrected. "Knowing we are likely looking for a Glock is a plus. The fact that it's a popular model, not so much." I sipped my coffee. "Since the 2015 open-carry law, though, knowing it might be someone who had a concealed-carry doesn't help us to terribly much."

"Stupid law," Vasily said with heat.

"Now, now, Detective," I laughed wryly. "Don't cast aspersions on our noble legislators."

"Whatever," he snorted. "At least *mine* didn't vote for it."

I tried not to chuckle again. "You've lived here nearly as long as California," I reminded him. "They are your legislators as much as mine now."

"Once a Californian..."

Rolling my eyes, I continued my earlier thought. "We're doubly handicapped by being barred from having a gun registry of any kind. Pull a list of possible gun shops that are a reasonable drive from Windeport; depending on what you turn up, maybe we can warrant our way to a sales list and get lucky."

"I thought you might say that," Vasily said as he flipped something on his tablet. "Assuming someone would go as far south as Portland, as far west as Augusta, and perhaps as far north as Bangor, there are about fifteen reputable places one could purchase the models we are after."

"It's a small enough list to start with," I nodded. "Get a warrant--"

"Already sitting on the judge's desk. I should hear within the hour."

"Not bad," I nodded approvingly.

"Once it's approved, I'll have Mark do the first round of calls. Lydia's on patrol today."

"How about the Coroner's report?" I asked as I wandered to the window and stared out at the field. The early physical education classes were out running up and down the field, bundled in layers of sweats against the sudden cold snap.

"This is where it gets interesting," he said, his voice vibrating with excitement. "Time of death couldn't be determined exactly."

"What?" I said, turning. "Why?"

"When the van arrived, the techs took the liver temp and it seemed anomalous. So, they took it again about forty minutes later and it had only dropped a fraction of a degree."

"Equipment failure?" I started to ask, and then snapped my fingers. "Damn. The water bottles."

Vasily nodded. "They appear to have insulated the body, or at least the torso, against the overnight chill - not that it was strictly necessary. The last few nights have been fairly warm, which also messed with their math. Maude in the ME's office is running a backup set of tests now, but she's thinking he might have been shot far, far earlier than we realized."

"Circumstances led us to think around eight or so on Sunday, right?"

"Yeah. It's more likely it was mid-afternoon."

"Shit," I swore. "We were looking at *lunch* on the table, not dinner."

"Exactly."

I sipped my coffee and inexplicably suddenly craved a sweetener for it. "Someone shot him midday Sunday?" I asked. "How is it that no one saw him out there?"

"There are twelve houses on that street," Vasily said. "Patrol knocked on all of them, and only one - Sylvia - is actually there. The rest are already in Florida for the winter or were summer rentals and have been closed up for the season."

"Curiouser and curiouser," I said. "This was definitely planned."

Vasily nodded. "Yep. We can add premeditated to our list of issues." He scrolled again. "Single gunshot, entry point definitely the mouth, bullet exited via..." he looked up. "Well, suffice it to say that he wouldn't have felt falling into the bed of the truck."

"That's about the only positive thing you've told me so far."

"Blood was all his. Stomach contents indicated he'd had two beers and more than a few spoonsful of beans and franks. Interestingly, they found evidence of advanced pancreatic cancer."

"Really?"

"Yeah, final stages. He had just a few weeks left. A month at most."

"Holy hell."

"Toxicology is pending. No other trace evidence - nothing under the nails, etcetera. No evidence of anyone else."

"Divers never found the gun in the cove, right?" I asked, circling back to the bullet.

"No. And we retraced our search in the neighborhood one more time and came up empty again."

I nodded. "That confirms, then, that the shooter took it with them. It goes with the nature of the crime scene. What about Heather's report?"

Vasily tapped his tablet. "About what you expected. House was clean of prints save for the one set on the door; she ran it through their databases and no hits. Nothing on the Fed's system either."

"That just tells us the shooter hasn't been caught before."

"Exactly." He scrolled. "I've got the inventory here and her photos of the scene. I'll put them in the investigation share for you."

"Thanks."

"One last thing," he said. "I was able to confirm *parts* of the financial situation."

I nodded. I'd emailed him what Charlie had told me about the mortgages on the bungalow; that was my final bit of work before I settled in to watch Miraculous Ladybug.

"Pelletier took out a mortgage on the house three years ago, to the tune of three hundred thousand dollars," Vasily said. "Last year, after the village did it's re-evaluation, he obtained a home equity line of credit for another two hundred thousand."

I nearly dropped my mug. "The house is worth half a million?"

"Six-hundred-eighty, actually," Vasily said. "Waterfront is desirable, especially a bungalow with deeded access to the water. Most of the homes in that area are investments now anyway and are used as rentals."

"Wow."

"Yeah. I'll check with Elaine, though. I don't think it's listed for anything close to that now."

"Interesting. Tell me what you find on that front." I sipped at the mug again. "Let's also run down anything on his bank accounts, credit cards, investments and such. I have a hunch I know what we'll find but it would be worth looking. I especially want to know if he bought those water jugs."

"On that last part, Heather noted they were from a delivery service. It might be easier to track it from that side."

"Okay."

"As for the other financials, we're going to have to go through the estate now, right? I don't imagine the bank is going to turn over anything without a warrant or permission."

"Yeah."

"I'll check with Dean and Smithwick," Vasily said, referring to the only law firm in town. "If he didn't go through them, they'll be able to point me to other likely firms."

"Sounds good." I paused, putting my coffee mug down on the desk and leaning on the back of my chair. "I want to head over to the University to follow the money trail, but before we go, Charlie told me you'd done some... research on Deidre."

Vasily looked at me and I could tell he was trying to divine whether I was angry with him. "Yes," he said after a few moments. "I'd heard the rumors about the IGA and confirmed with Elaine that it was actually on the market. You'd not mentioned it to me, so I... got worried, frankly."

"Go on."

He swallowed hard. "I didn't bring this to you initially, Sean, because you're my friend - my *best* friend," he said with emphasis before looking away.

"You could have come to me with this," I said reasonably.

"I... didn't want you to get hurt," he continued, which seemed like an odd phrase from him. "The more I dug, the more I discovered just how much of a clean break Deidre had decided on. And... I thought you'd not be all that happy I was looking into your girlfriend."

"I'm not upset, Vasily," I said softly. "It is a bit irregular, I'll grant you that," I sighed, "but whatever you've found might be the only closure I get. I pushed her out of my life; I suppose I don't deserve any more than that."

He looked back at me. "She's marrying someone in Atlanta next month," he said simply.

That made me lean back on the windowsill as though I'd taken a punch to the gut. "No shit."

"Yeah. I almost missed it, but the proceeds from the sale of the IGA went into a new joint account with her and a—" he looked at the tablet "--uh, Thomas Feldman? A cross-name search brought me to the wedding announcement."

"Shit," I said again. "Please tell me it's not Thomas Feldman, the quarterback?"

"Yeah," he nodded. "Class ahead of you, wasn't he?"

"Yes," I nodded back. "He was a jerk twenty years ago. Total football jock. Deidre had dated him for a bit then parted ways when he was drafted and became a benchwarmer in Oakland."

"He's a successful building contractor now," Vasily said, looking at his tablet. "Has two kids from a prior marriage."

"Ah," I said sadly. "There it is."

"Yeah," he said.

"So, when she was going to Boston, she wasn't, was she?"

"No," he replied. "She's been visiting him in Atlanta for about eighteen months; more regularly since May of this year."

I felt numb again. "I had no reason to verify," I said quietly. "Why? When I called her, she answered. Cell phones have a way of making you feel more connected than you are, I suppose."

Vasily stood and came around toward me, and tentatively put a hand to my shoulder. "I *am* sorry, dude," he said going full Californian on me. "It's a sucky way to lose your lover."

"Thanks," I smiled. "I'll survive. I'm not the first to have been left in the dust by someone."

"True," he said, lingering for a moment before squeezing my shoulder as he returned to the other side of the desk. "But if you want to talk about it, I'm here for you."

"That means a lot. Thanks."

"I'll get my things and meet you in the SUV."

"Vasily - one second."

He turned at my door, a partial smile on his face. "Chief?"

I looked at him carefully, wondering if my timing was right and sighed. When it rained, it poured, right? "So... Father sold the building out from beneath us."

"Oh," Vasily said, and his face took on a hard expression.

"Yeah. He's drawn some conclusions based on our living arrangements. Apparently, that motivated him to sell everything."

"Bastard," Vasily breathed. "If I—"

"Temper, temper," I laughed, cutting off his tirade.

"When do we have to be out?" he asked, anger nipping at his words.

"The fifteenth," I said. "But I have an idea, and you're obviously welcome to stay with me once I get everything arranged."

"Can I help in any way?"

"Let me see how this plays out. If I truly get all my rent money back, I might be okay." I walked up to him and put my own hand on his shoulder. "Besides, there's no way I'd charge my closest friend rent."

He smiled warmly. "Dude—"

"It's nothing. Now go, I'll meet you outside in about twenty."

"All right," he said and vanished through the door.

As I walked back to the window behind my desk, I pulled out my iPhone and dialed a number. "Elaine? It's Sean. I'm in a bit of a pickle and I think you might be able to help me..."

Nineteen

Despite the water heater being on the fritz at the station, I managed to run through the shower and get to the SUV just when I said I would; we arrived in front of the College of Agriculture a little after nine and proceeded to park in the red zone once more. Vasily followed me up to the business office, where we found Barbara Thompson typing away at, of all things, an IBM Selectric Typewriter.

"Barb," I said as I pushed through the glass door. "What the Hell?"

She looked up at me, over the rims of her glasses. "I know, right? But the Travel Office still requires forms in triplicate, and damn it, the laser printer just doesn't do it right." She patted the side of the sky-blue case affectionately. "Bessie and I have been through a lot, and she's yet to let me down."

"Bessie? Really?"

"Don't judge, Chief," she chuckled. "What can I do for you this morning?"

"You mentioned when I spoke with you on Monday that funding had been tight."

"Still is," she said. "I'm not sure we'll make it through this fiscal year with the staff intact. We can't cut faculty of course - tenure rules and all - but to be honest, we're already a bit thin. Another whack and I'll be the business manager for the entire college."

"That sounds... horrible."

"Won't matter. I'm retiring in May. Screw Bedard," she smiled.

"Tell me how you really feel, Barb," I laughed.

She laughed again. "I've been here a long, long time, Chief. It's time for a change."

"I keep hearing that from people," I said, my eyes catching Vasily's for a moment. "Florida, is it?"

"Nah," she replied as she rolled the paper out of the typewriter and searched for a pen on her desk. "My sister has a duplex outside of Phoenix. I'm headed West."

"Good for you," I smiled. "Look, if I recall how university finances work, you have access to the accounts and the budget for the entire college, right?"

"I do."

"Do you also have the specific sources of that funding?"

"Sort of," she said. "State funding is pretty transparent, though we have far fewer dollars from them now than when I started back during the Pleistocene. Now we rely heavily on grants or endowments, or the occasional philanthropic donation."

"What's the percentage?" Vasily asked. He'd once again slipped out his notebook and had been jotting down our conversation.

"Damn, I'd have to say dollars from the beneficent legislature make maybe fifteen percent now?" She turned to her computer. "Hang on, I just did our quarterly report for Bedard... yeah, here it is. Fifteen from State, about thirty from grants, and this past year, the balance was in private donations."

"Can you tell if the grants are from the Extension?"

Barb looked at me and nodded. "LaChance's funding?"

"Exactly."

She punched some keys on her computer. "No," she frowned. "Oddly, his accounts are Foundation-based, so I don't have access to the underlying data." She looked back to me. "That only means his money came from 'other than university sources,' though. Could be the Extension, could be donations."

I looked to Vasily. "Sounds like another stop," I said.

"Yeah," Barb said thoughtfully. "But you won't get far without a bit of help," she added.

"What do you mean?"

"Those goobers are notoriously secretive," she chuckled. "They guard their fundraising lists like they are the Dead Sea Scrolls."

"I'll take what help I can get," I said, narrowing my eyes. "But I can get a warrant if I need it."

"That'll take too long," she said. "Believe me. They once froze out the Bangor Daily on an FOIA request - five years."

My eyes widened. "Wow. Okay then."

Barb rolled her chair backwards. "Michael!" she hollered.

"Yeah," came a muffled reply from a back room in the corner. I could vaguely hear the humming of some sort of equipment, something I'd missed before.

"Get out here, kid."

"Do I have too, Miss Thompson?" came a rather plaintive reply. "I'm not done with the Scantron run for Dr. Phelp's class."

"You're on my dime, Mike. Get out here."

"Yes, ma'am," came a very reluctant reply.

A moment later, a tall kid dressed in an oversized hoodie and matching sweats slowly walked out of the back room; he had his head down slightly, hiding his face and emphasizing how unhappy he was to have been called away from his work. Hands shoved into his pockets, he stopped beside Barbara's desk.

"One second," she said as she rolled another piece of paper into the typewriter. Amazingly, her hands started to fly over the ancient typewriter's keys while she continued to talk. "I want you to take these two gentlemen over to Phyllis at the Foundation—"

A strangled cry issued from the recesses of the hoodie. "Miss Thompson! Please—!"

"Mike," Barb said gently, "I promised to help you and I will - Sam will be here once you get back. This is important; Chief Colbeth is working on Dr. Pelletier's case."

"He is?"

"Yes. I can't leave, but you can. Take them the back way. I'll call ahead and Phyllis will meet you." She put a hand to his arm. "No one should see you other than Phyllis and the Chief."

"You can count on our discretion, Mike," I said, wondering why on earth it mattered.

I understood as soon as the undergrad turned and faced me fully, for he was wearing an awfully familiar mask on his face; I suspected the hood was covering other sins, such as two cat ears. "All right," he said.

"Thank you," I said warmly.

"That should do it," Barbara said, and she rolled the paper out of the typewriter, grabbed her pen, and signed it with a flourish. Holding it to Mike, she continued. "This is for Phyllis, and it's from the Dean. Make sure she follows it to the letter."

Pausing slightly to look at us again, Mike quickly retrieved the letter and stuffed it back into his pocket, but not before I saw the telltale claw tips.

"Are you going to be in trouble for this?" I asked Barbara.

"No," she chuckled. "I know where all of the bodies are. That gives me asbestos panties."

Vasily choked; I felt the same way but managed to keep the image out of my mind as I smiled. "Thanks. I owe you."

"I know," she laughed.

I turned to Mike who was hovering by a side exit. "Lead the way, my friend."

He bowed and we trailed behind him down a back hallway of the office. "I don't often get to take this route," he said somewhat happily as we moved through a cubicle farm. "We used to store a lot of stuff down there, but Miss Thompson has digitized most of it."

"Down?" Vasily asked.

"Yeah," Michael turned slightly. "It's officially the first floor of the building, but it's really the basement. We call it the bat cave."

I looked at Vasily. "Holy shit, they're real," I said.

Michael laughed. "The tunnels? Yep. It's the fastest way to get between buildings, especially during the winter."

"I thought they were only a rumor," Vasily said. "All the jokes about Deans and their girlfriends...?"

"Some are true," Michael confirmed, feeling more comfortable with us. "I've not seen it, but my buddy over in Accounting accidentally found the Vice-Dean—"

"Uh, maybe we shouldn't hear this," I advised.

Michael's head snapped around, and this time I did hear the tiny tinkle of a bell. "You won't tell anyone I said that, right? This gig is part of my work-study program," he added, a bit of worry on what I could see of his expression.

"No," I said. "You're officially helping my investigation," I added, "so *everything* you say or do with us is protected."

Vasily shot me a look but prudently remained quiet.

Michael seemed to breathe a bit easier. "Okay, cool."

Our trio reached a nondescript door, and Michael turned slightly. "One second," he muttered. "I need my ID... damn it..." he swore, then shot a look back at us before lifting his sweatshirt slightly to get to one of the two pockets on the front of his costume. Unzipping one, he produced a university ID badge that he pressed to the RFID reader beside the door; the light switched from red to green and the door clicked open.

As he held the door for us, he groaned, and seemed to come to a decision. Once the door clicked shut behind us, he paused at the top of the industrial steps and turned to face both of us. "Okay, so this is embarrassing."

"I'm a police officer," I smiled. "Believe me, I've seen it all."

Mike looked at us again. "So, I was at a party last night with my girlfriend. There's this show she's really into—"

"Miraculous Ladybug."

His eyes widened. "You know it?"

"I do now," I laughed. "I was Chat Noir last night at the *Not-So-Scary Party* held at the Library."

"Seriously!" he breathed. "Wow. Epic."

"There was even a Ladybug, too."

"Yeah, that's what Amy wanted to go as," Mike replied as we started down the steps. "Anyway, I ordered this costume off of the internet, and totally impressed her — it was a surprise, really — and the party was great, you know?"

"I'm getting the picture," I laughed. At the bottom of the steps, Mike palmed another reader, and we entered a roundish corridor made of concrete. Industrial lights bathed the space in a washed out white.

"Well, one thing led to another," Mike continued, "and, well, without going into details..."

"Probably wise," Vasily said.

"Uh... yeah..." Mike replied. The tunnel turned to the left, and then opened into a four-way intersection. He turned to the left and we followed. "I guess, technically, I didn't sleep last night..." he laughed a bit nervously. "Anyway, I lost track of time. I had to get to work, but when I tried to change out of the costume, the zipper got stuck."

"That could be a problem," I said. "If yours is anything like mine."

"Yeah," he said as we paused again at the bottom of another set of stairs. "I spent so long trying to get out of it that I didn't have time to pull the ears or mask. Hence the sweats."

"You wore this... all night?" I asked.

"Yeah," he said, and what I could see of his face flamed a bit. "We were... cosplaying after the party."

"Cosplay--?" I looked at Vasily who nodded like he understood. I followed his lead and replied, simply, "Well, it *was* Halloween."

"Yeah. Miss Thompson has a friend in the theater department that will hopefully be able to help; I spent a lot on this costume and would prefer not to ruin it."

Wondering once more how much my own version of Chat Noir had cost Charlie, I nodded. "I might also know someone who can help," I said. "If Miss Thompson gives us leave, I'll take you to her." I paused. "On the down low, of course."

"Thanks," he smiled. "This way."

The other side of the door at the top of the stairwell was a small room with a window facing a grassy field. Two small chairs were stacked in the corner and an empty bookcase was on the wall. "Wait here," Mike said. "I need to finesse Phyllis and it might be easier without the two of you standing behind me."

"Sounds like a plan," I agreed. "But a word of advice?"

He looked at me, expectantly. "Sure."

"Put the hood down. I've recently discovered that women go crazy over the ears."

Mike's eyes widened behind the mask. "Really?"

"Yes," I nodded sagely.

"Okay," he said, and tentatively he pulled the hood down to expose a mop of wildly disheveled blond hair, with two triangular feline ears perched just so. It took a moment for me to realize the hair wasn't a wig. "I'll be right back."

Vasily couldn't take it any longer and started to chortle the moment Mike was out of earshot. "The poor kid!" he laughed. "And how did you know about the ears?"

"I guessed," I smiled. "Suzanne kept looking at them last night."

"You learn fast."

"Yep." I wandered to the window. "Do I want to know what 'cosplaying' is?"

"Only if you are planning on pursuing Suzanne," Vasily laughed. "From what I saw last night, she looks to be a member of that community."

"Community? *Seriously*?"

"You are so naive," Vasily chortled again.

"Clearly," I said just as my phone buzzed. I glanced at the text. "Caitlyn got us an appointment with the managing partner at Dean and Smithwick."

"Managing partner? They are that big?"

"No," I laughed. "Frank has an ego large enough to inflate the size of the firm on that alone." I looked up. "Two o'clock."

"Okay," Vasily said just as we heard a distinctive jingle approach from the hallway.

Michael skidded to a stop in front of us, holding a wad of paper in a gloved hand and catching his breath. "Got it," he said, handing me the paper. "And you were right! Phyllis couldn't take her eyes off the ears and never read the letter Miss Thompson gave me."

"Nice work," I said, looking at the time on my phone and then speed dialing Charlie. "Now, let's see if we can't get you out of that costume safely..."

Twenty

We made a quick side trip to Michael's dorm room to retrieve some street clothes before driving over to Charlie's rambling farmhouse on the outskirts of town. Given how late she'd been at the Library the night before, she'd pulled rank and taken the day off. Fortunately, that meant we'd be able to drop in on her to make good on my promise to the twenty-something undergrad.

It wasn't a long ride, but long enough that Michael and Vasily swapped various theories on the show they both appeared to follow in great detail. I'd never been attached to anything in pop culture, so it was a bit eye opening to find people so invested in something as seemingly simplistic as an animated show. And yet, what little I was able to follow led me to believe it had characters and depth equal to some of the best novels I'd ever read. Clearly, I needed to bond with my Netflix when I had some downtime.

Charlie met us on her front porch, watching as I drove up the rutted drive in the SUV. The white clapboard farmhouse dated back to the founding of the town, though despite having a barn, was no longer used actively for agriculture. Shutting down the SUV, the three of us exited and walked to the steps.

"Nice ears," Charlie said as we approached. "Come with me," she said as she wrapped an arm around the faux feline. "We'll make this right as rain. There's chili in the crockpot if you're hungry," she added as we followed her in. "Bowls and fixings are on the sideboard."

"We didn't come to crash lunch," I said defensively, though my stomach – traitor that it was – chose that moment to rumble loudly.

"You're not," she laughed. "It's leftover from last night."

She went toward what I knew was her den, and I headed the other way toward the massive kitchen in the rear. I'd spent a lot of time there since childhood, as the house had been in Charlie's family for decades. Even though her mom – my Aunt - now lived in a small apartment close to her restaurant over on Route One, we still gathered for Family Dinner most Sundays in that cozy space. No one would ever get me to admit publicly how much I looked forward to my time with my nieces each weekend.

As promised, the crockpot was sitting on the butcher block; generously sized bowls with spoons were beside it, as well as several smaller bowls with add ins like onions, cheddar cheese and crackers. The smell was divine, and I suspected now that Charlie herself had cooked much of the food on offer last night at the party.

Handing a bowl to Vasily, I mused a bit. "Today's Thursday? I think I want to make an unannounced visit to the *Journal* tomorrow. It would be nice to know what Pelletier said to the editor."

"I should have time to run through the financials we just got after we meet with the lawyers," Vasily said as he scooped a massive amount of chili into his bowl. "Are we staying over again?" he asked.

"Maybe," I said. "But if we do, not at the Ritz this time, sadly."

"Understood," he smiled as I moved behind him to fill my bowl, and then took a seat at the massive wooden table ringed with Shaker-style chairs. "Man, this smells fantastic."

"I didn't get a chance to try it last night," I admitted. "I was… distracted."

"Yes, you were," Vasily laughed.

We settled into a companionable silence while we plowed through two bowls each of Charlie's Chili. As we crept closer to one-thirty, though, I started to worry that something had gone wrong with the extraction, and carefully made my way to the den.

I knocked at the closed door. "Charlie?"

"C'mon in," she said.

I slid one of the two doors open and found her at the sewing table, a pin in her mouth and the Chat costume on the table. "Uh, oh," I said as I watched her rhythmically repair what looked like a separation along the zipper seam.

"Not as bad as it looks," she said, glancing up at me. "Mike's in the shower. The eye black he used didn't come off easily with the makeup remover wipes I had, and I'm also hoping the hot water will loosen the glue he used on the mask."

"Wow."

"Yeah. Poor kid. He took the first video he found on YouTube."

"Not unusual for that generation."

"No kidding," she laughed. "They tend to Google first and *then* come to Library when they get called out for it by their professors."

Unintentionally, the detective in me took the opportunity to scan the room, and my eyes fell on the gun safe in the corner. Trying to sound casual, I asked: "I thought you got rid of that after David died?"

"Mm hmm?" she said, and then followed my gaze. "Oh, *that*. No; as it's been in my husband's family for ages, I've not quite been up to calling St. Catherine's Auxiliary to have them add it to their annual rummage sale."

"David's been gone for a while, Charlie," I said softly.

"I know," she said as her eyes connected with mine, and for a moment, I could see her pain from the loss of her soulmate was still keen. David had been like an older brother to me; I'd spent many an afternoon after one of Charlie's fabulous Sunday Family Dinners playing cribbage, talking politics and keeping half an ear on whatever Boston sports team happened to be on the radio. "Someday. Maybe," she shrugged.

"Good. No reason to keep it, especially if you don't have any guns."

"Who says I don't?" she chuckled good naturedly, trying to erase the sudden chill I'd brought to the space.

"*Charlie!*" I exclaimed, unable to stop myself. "You have *kids* in the house!"

"And a locked safe," she replied, pausing mid-stitch to look up at me. "What's this about?"

"Nothing," I said. "Just my natural protective tendencies."

Charlie didn't seem convinced, but I also knew I couldn't push much further without forcing my hand. A moment later, she held up the costume, allowing the bell-zipper to ding as she did so. "There!" she said. "I replaced the crappy zipper this came with and swapped out the Velcro for his baton with something better."

"You did all of that? In an hour?"

"When you're good, you're good," she laughed as she carefully zipped the costume closed and then folded it up. She put the two feline ears on top, and then set them next to the boots and belt tail that were already waiting on the counter.

"Thank you," I said. "Believe it or not, he was quite helpful earlier. The ears especially."

"He told me," she replied.

We both looked up when there was a knock at the open door. Mike was there in somewhat normal attire - t-shirt and jeans. His hair was still damp from the shower and flying away at all angles and held the black domino mask in one hand. "I put the towels in the hamper," he said. "It took a bit, but the gum adhesive finally loosened."

Charlie turned and plucked a small container off her counter, then handed it to Mike. "Use this next time," she said. "Removes with just a dab of alcohol."

"I can't take this," he said.

"Of course you can," she laughed. "And if you need any alterations, you come right back to me." She packed up the costume into a shopping bag and handed it to Mike. "Tell your friends. I'm at the Library so you can't miss me."

"There's chili in the kitchen," I said. "Grab a bite and then we'll run you back to campus."

"Okay," he smiled. "Thanks!" The transformation from mask-wearing superhero to ordinary looking undergrad was amazing; I'd have been hard pressed to have said he was — what did Vasily call it? A cosplayer? He seemed very ordinary.

Then again, as I watched him turn and head for the kitchen, something he's said in the tunnel suddenly struck me. I put a pin in it and turned back to Charlie. "Chili was awesome. And next year, I'll help you with the cooking."

"I don't need—"

"Yes, you do," I said as I swooped in to hug her. "I'm not sure the town knows that you are single handedly pulling off this and all of the parties we have at the Library."

"I don't do it for the recognition," she said curtly.

"I know," I laughed. "But you'll have my help. Whether you like it or not, Cousin."

Despite herself, she smiled. "Thanks."

Wandering back to the kitchen, I found Vasily polishing off *another* bowl and deep in discussion with Mike on some finer point of... something. I cleared my throat. "Mike," I said when they both stopped and looked up. "Who was Dr. Pelletier seeing?"

The color drained from the kid's face, and he looked between me and Vasily. "I'm... I'm not sure I know what you're asking," he said. But his eyes were wide with fear.

"Hey, I get it," I said as I slid into a chair across from them. "Student workers are there to work in the background. Seen but not heard." I snagged a cracker from Vasily. "But they also see everything. And often, the faculty and staff they work with forget they are there."

Mike swallowed.

"You must have been surprised, given how old he was," I smiled, popping the cracker into my mouth.

Mike stared at me. "I was," he said after a long moment.

Taking another shot in the dark, I stole one more cracker from Vasily before asking: "What did Barbara say when you told her?"

Mike flushed a bit. "She caught me when I bolted out of the stairwell. And she knew something was wrong; I had to tell her what I'd seen. Miss Thompson figured it started after he lost his wife; we all knew Dr. Pelletier was quite lonely." Suddenly, his eyes lit up with a bit of anger, and I realized he'd likely picked that up from Barbara. "Dean Bedard suddenly started fussing over him last year, and I heard through the grapevine they'd gone out of state together a few times. I didn't believe it; she's a bi—" he caught himself.

"Yes," I smiled. "She is. Go on."

Swallowing again, Mike continued. "It was back in late August. We'd just returned from summer break and I was in the bat cave, returning from dropping some paperwork off at Admin for Miss Thompson." He paused, then smiled. "Actually, I might start calling it the 'Chat Cave' now, seeing I was down there in costume."

"Knock yourself out," Vasily laughed.

"Anyway, I rounded that final curve and nearly ran over the two of them. They were..." he flushed, while simultaneously looking disgusted. "Well, doing the nasty against the wall."

My eyes widened. "Bedard?" I said incredulously, shooting a glance at an equally disturbed Vasily. "And Pelletier?"

"Yeah," he said, gulping. "Fortunately, they didn't hear me, and I backed away from them. There's another stairway on the southeastern side of the building."

"That was August?" I asked.

"Yes. A few weeks later, Pelletier stopped coming to his office. We all assumed he was avoiding Dean Bedard."

"Thanks," I said, looking back at Vasily. "Now, finish up that chili and we'll get you back to campus."

Twenty-One

We had little time to discuss the amazing discovery of the Bedard-Pelletier hookup before our meeting with Frank Smithwick to try and get access to the estate's finances. The law firm was housed in one of the former summer vacation mansions on the Sea Road, perfectly pretentious looking with filigree everywhere and two-tone paint instead of the normal whitewashed clapboards. The drive was semicircular and had space for several cars; as I parked the SUV, it appeared to be a slow day at the office, for only Frank's red Cadillac was there.

Entrance was gained via the magnificent grand portico, but the reception desk nestled into the massive Hollywood staircase hovering over the foyer was empty. "Hello?" I called out, hearing my voice echo.

"In here, Chief," came a voice off to our left.

We turned and walked down a short hallway that opened into what might have been the formal dining room in another era; as befitting Frank's worldview, it was his office, with a desk just in front of the massive windows fronting the street. He stood and came around, holding out his hand. "Sean," he smiled.

"Frank," I replied, shaking his hand. "Light staff day?"

"Lunch hour," he said, though even with the smile, it had the ring of a lie to it.

"Ah," I said. "Well," I continued as we sat, "I need a favor."

"All right. Shoot."

I tried not to frown at his turn of phrase. "I'm looking into Ingmar

Pelletier's death. I'd like access to his banking records to run down a few items that have drawn our attention."

"Such as?"

"Obviously, I can't tell you that, Frank," I smiled. "Are you handling the estate?"

Frank continued to smile. "Yes," he said. "Ingmar has been a client for years."

"Would you be willing to allow us access to the finances of the estate?"

"You should really get a warrant," Frank said. How he was able to keep the smile up was beyond me.

"I should," I nodded. "But it would take time, and things are moving fast. We have a short window and I'm worried we might miss it."

Frank considered me, and I wondered idly how much he spent on teeth whitening. Smiling the way he did made me think it was substantial. "I don't know... it would be irregular in the extreme."

"Who is the executor? Should we talk to them?"

"The firm is filling that role," he said. "Ingmar didn't have any kids, and all of his siblings predeceased him."

"No nephews? Nieces?" For some reason, I flashed on Deidre's desire for kids; seeing the result of not having any - or having siblings that had them - was a bit sobering.

"None."

"So, the decision rests with you, then," I pointed out.

"Yes."

I looked at him, and realized other than the threat of a warrant, I had no real leverage. Nothing I could use in a horse trade for information - not that I could anyway, for I needed to procure the evidence properly. Anything I obtained in a manner that could be viewed as questionable in court would damage the ultimate case we would build.

So, I smiled. It was all I had.

Frank seemed to read into my smile, and maybe thought he saw some desperation on my part. That wasn't far from the truth, for what we had at this point was pretty limited. Slowly, Frank started to nod. "I don't see why not," he said. "How far back?"

"Five years," Vasily said. "Bank accounts, credit cards, investments."

"I'll have it to the station for you by the end of the day," Frank said as he stood. His smile seemed to have shifted; I read it to say *you owe me.*

I smiled back. "Thank you," I said as I shook his hand, my smile pleasantly saying *eat dirt.*

Twenty-Two

Back at the station, I was standing at the window once more watching the late afternoon unspool over the athletic fields of the high school. It was well after three and it appeared that the soccer team had a game on the lower field; I wasn't entirely certain, but the upper field seemed to be the start/finish line for the cross-country team. By any standard, a busy afternoon for the athletic director.

Something was bothering me; well, technically, the entire case was bothering me, but I didn't have enough data to form even a mild hypothesis. All I had was Ingmar Pelletier's dead body, and a ton of unrelated information. Asking questions had only provided *more* seemingly unrelated connections. All I knew to do at this point was to keep asking questions, keep poking around the edges until firmer picture emerged.

Experience had taught me that would ultimately be a good thing. But for some reason, I was chafing at my own normal patterns and practices. And still, on top of all of *that*, something was bothering me.

I sipped from my mug, having long lost track of how much coffee I'd consumed so far, and pondered. Up on the athletic field, one of the girls clad in the colors of the school broke away and took the soccer ball all the way down the field; her shot went well wide of the goal. It seemed a bit like a metaphor for the case: killing Ingmar hadn't made sense initially, and now having a possible circle of suspects didn't make it any more reasonable than before.

Yet, clearly, it had been planned. The timing spoke to that; the water bottles, which Vasily was running down as I watched the soccer game, were also signs that someone had plotted out nearly every detail. If we'd not found the bullet —

I stopped, mid sip. If the murder had happened mid-day, whoever did it would have to have been in and out quickly. I was reasonably comfortable thinking it was someone Ingmar knew, but even so, whoever it was wouldn't have stuck around long after having shot him. I went back to my desk and flipped through Heather's report on the carport, confirming that there had been no tool marks around the bullet. That meant we had been the first to locate it.

I flipped more pages in the report, nodding. The shell casing for the shot hadn't been retrieved by us. If he'd been shot in the bed of the truck... where would they have stood? No, not stood, maybe kneeled? On the tailgate? I scanned the report again, but Heather was silent on that aspect. More to the point, though, was the simple fact that the casing *had* been collected, which Ingmar himself would have not been able to do; it must have ejected oddly, and had taken long enough to locate that there had been no time to retrieve the bullet itself. Removing both would have hampered us immeasurably, so that was the first mistake made. Understanding now that there might have been time constraints may have resulted in others we'd not seen — yet.

That also spoke to it being someone who knew they would be recognized. My eyes flicked to the whiteboard in the corner of my office, where several names had been written: Bedard. LaChance. Gauthier. They were all connected to Pelletier in one way or another, though I still had no clear understanding of a motive *any* of them might have to see the professor dead.

And I knew all of them, personally.

This was going to get more uncomfortable the more digging I did.

Flipping to the coroner's report, I re-confirmed there was residual GSR on Ingmar's hands, but my assumption from the beginning had been that he'd had his hands pressed to the gun but had not necessarily pulled the trigger. However, there wasn't a conclusive way to *prove* that.

Our teams had been over the house multiple times, so it was unlikely we had missed the brass. But it might be worth one more search. Sipping my now tepid coffee, I returned to the window and the soccer match. The brass would only confirm exactly what kind of bullet had been used, though there was a chance the firing pin on the gun used might have a particular mark. Without anything to compare it to, though, finding the shell casing wouldn't get me much at this point.

There was a soft knock at my door. "Chief?"

I turned to see Vasily. "Hey."

He wandered in and sat on the edge of my desk, something no other subordinate did. "I did an end-about run on Frank and called Poland Springs. Ingmar wasn't a regular customer."

"All right," I said. "That doesn't surprise me, since we already determined there was no cooler."

"True. But I played a hunch," he said, his eyes dancing.

"Don't make me drag it out of you, *Detective*," I warned.

"Sorry," he said. "I asked if anyone in the neighborhood was a customer and if they'd had a delivery. We've already interviewed her, and she never mentioned she was missing her water."

"Sylvia?" I asked.

"Yeah. Last delivery was a few weeks ago. If you remember the report—"

I held up a finger as I scrolled my iPad to the crime photos, then zoomed in. "How many do they normally deliver?"

"Ten."

I counted the bottles surrounding the body. Two were empty out of nine. I looked up. "One is in the cooler?"

"Has to be."

"Please tell me these bottles have tracking numbers."

"Yep," he smiled grimly as he showed me his display. "They match what was delivered to fifteen Ocean View Avenue two weeks ago."

"Damn. Get over there *now* and take Mark or Lydia with you; I'll call a judge for a warrant as a backup, but Probable Cause should get us through the door."

"On it," he said as I picked up the phone to call the court in our district.

"Shit," I said to no one in particular.

Twenty-Three

Inexplicably, Sylvia had suddenly taken some vacation time and had left her staff to deal with the back end of the Symposium as it wrapped up. My brief conversation with her boss at the Colonial left me unsettled; she'd told him it was a family emergency, and she'd be back as soon as she could be. That meant a long night of dredging travel records to determine where she had gone - if we were lucky enough that she'd not tried to cover her tracks.

It was hard to believe she was fleeing Windeport, an action of a suspect; but the water bottles tied her to the scene of the crime. Even if she'd not seen the bed of the truck (which she had), the disappearance of nine five-gallon bottles from her house might have been worth mentioning.

But what was the motivation? Nothing I had uncovered so far made sense, which only meant I didn't have the full picture yet. I was tempted to throw my iPad across the room, but instead opted for a walk down the block for a fresh cup of coffee at Calista's.

Getting the expedited search warrant hadn't been an issue, and Vasily had picked it up on the way over to Sylvia's house. With her being absent, locating the last remaining water bottle had been a trivial exercise and it had only taken a few moments beyond that to match the tracking number with Poland Spring's customer records. I'd had the presence of mind to include locating the Glock we suspected had been used in the murder as part of our warrant, which meant it would be a bit before Vasily and our patrol officers returned.

Exiting the station, I zipped my fleece up against the chilly afternoon and bent against the breeze that was swirling the remains of the leaves that the town public works folks had missed. Route One was quiet, and for a moment I considered the empty storefronts as I made my way up the street. In the late Fall gloom, the town felt as dead as the maple trees running along the street. I tried to imagine what it had been like back when fishing was king and the rich from Boston flocked to the seashore; it was hard to reconcile that past with a census that indicated we'd lost nearly a quarter of our population in the last count. I feared the next count would be worse.

I crossed a side street and passed the old pharmacy, pausing for a moment at the massive plate glass windows that had once displayed the special of the week. Mom had always done a traditional holiday window, just like the big department stores in New York; the lack of one the year she'd passed had been something I'd felt acutely. My eyes fell on the soda fountain that was still there, and the pharmacy counter beyond, and remembered fondly after-school sessions with a fresh root beer float served with love.

As I looked at the dusty counter, it occurred to me I'd spent many of those afternoons with Charlie; she was quite a few years older, of course, but that hadn't stopped her from treating me like her own kid brother. Once swimming began to eat up the rest of my life, though, there had been less and less time for moments such as those; they ended abruptly when she departed for college – but not before a strong bond between us had been forged. I was sure that was why I went out of my way to be at her Sunday Dinners, for those afternoons at the soda fountain were memories I had long cherished.

It had been a different time, and now, somehow, everything had changed.

Pressing into the wind, I continued down the street and rounded the corner of Maple. Even at this hour, the parking lot was full, and a few hardy souls were sitting at the outside tables on the sidewalk. I nodded to one or two people I recognized, but was on autopilot; a few minutes later, I was back on the sidewalk with my cup brimming with the nectar of life. I dithered on the corner, though, and turned away from the station, continuing up the street toward the cathedral for St. Catherine by the Sea.

The spires weren't the tallest, strictly speaking, and the congregation had dwindled over the decades. These days, the current flock was all that remained from having combined with the sister church the next town over, and even that looked like it might not be enough to keep them going. I wasn't Catholic, but the space had always been a welcoming refuge to any and all, and I'd often found a quiet peace sitting inside the sanctuary and contemplating the stained glass.

I was between sessions when I quietly entered the sanctuary. The lights were dimmed, and candles were lit up in the narthex. I slid into a row toward the rear, well aware that Sister Margaret would be on my case should she discover me with my coffee. Again.

Could Sylvia be our murderer? I found myself shaking my head, but knew I needed to treat her as our primary suspect now. But Bedard's apparent romance of Ingmar was suspect, too. Given what little we knew already about the finances at the College of Agriculture, it appeared that Ingmar had been controlling the purse strings, somehow - Menard LaChance had alluded to that in his keynote, and Barbara had essentially confirmed it. I needed to pour through the paperwork from the Foundation, though, or better yet, have Vasily take a run at it. My friend and partner had a knack for uncovering the oddest things in the footnotes of an annual report.

I pressed a hand to my eyes. I also needed to get to Boston again; I probably didn't need to do a personal interview with Jordan but seeing someone's reactions in real time could only be done that way. Phone wouldn't do. And now we'd need to go after Sylvia. Maybe we'd catch a break on that one, but if not, it probably meant calling Jimmy and crying Uncle.

The threads were starting to diverge, and I just didn't have the staff to track all of them.

My phone buzzed, and I slid it out of my pocket and hurried out to the vestibule. "Chief Colbeth."

"Sean?" came a feminine voice.

"Suzanne?" I replied. Panicking, I looked at my watch; it was barely five.

"I've had a hell of a day and wondered if you'd mind drinks before dinner," she said.

"No," I said. "Same here, actually."

"Well," she said, and I could hear the smile in her voice, "you tell me yours, and I'll tell you mine."

"Deal," I laughed. "Hotel Desrosier or Millie's?"

"Desrosier sounds nice," she said. "I've only been there once so far."

"Be there in ten," I said.

"See you there!" she said as she hung up.

I hurried out of the church and hustled down the sidewalk; the sky grew darker, and it felt as though the temperature had dropped a few degrees. By the time I made it to the small Best Western-branded inn situated across from the Library, tiny snowflakes had started to fall. I pushed into the lobby, which itself seemed out of time: it was a perfect representation of what roadside motels such as Hotel Desrosier had been in the forties and early fifties. A small board full of pamphlets of local attractions stood beside the tiny reception desk, behind which was a traditional set of cubby holes - one for each of the sixty rooms.

A small stairwell led to the second floor, with a hallway beside it that gave to the rooms on the first. The far side of the space had a set of French doors, currently propped open, that led to the restaurant and bar. I found Suzanne sitting at a table for two facing the out-of-themed flat screen television that was tuned to the pre-game for Thursday Night Football.

"Who's playing?" I asked as I took the seat across from her.

"It's a throwaway game," she smiled as I took off my fleece. "Dolphins and Giants."

"Ah," I laughed.

The waitress arrived and held her platter against her hip, the order pad atop it. "Chief," she smiled.

"Hey Andrea," I said. "What's on tap tonight?"

"I still have some Sam Adams Octoberfest. Other than that, the usual suspects."

I rolled my eyes. "Really?"

"I have to do that," she laughed.

"Sam Adams it is," I said. "And a soft pretzel, please."

"Dijon or Ranch?"

"Dijon."

"Back in a flash," she said and moved to the next table.

"So," I said, eyes locking on to her blue ones. "Tell me about the wonders of modern medicine."

"There are none," she laughed. "That's about the size of it."

"That can't be true," I replied.

"Oh, it went to Hell about the time we added computers to everything," she laughed again.

"I think that is true for most industries," I said. "Even mine."

"I don't believe that," she said. "I mean, you can match DNA in hours now, right?"

"Only on television. The tests are faster now, of course, but they still take days."

"But you can run bullets through a wiz-bang system to match them to guns?"

I looked at her. "We can," I said. "I didn't know you were so interested in the process."

"I'm not," she said as she drained the last of what might have been a chardonnay and motioned to the waitress for another. "Just making conversation."

I looked at her and noticed, finally, that she was tapping a well-manicured finger against the Formica top, then saw the slightly glazed eyes and realized it hadn't been her first glass of wine, either. "Suze," I said, unsure if we'd progressed to nicknames yet, "this wasn't just a bad day at the office, was it?"

She turned toward me, her rich hair moving in a subtle wave as she did so. "No," she admitted.

I slid my chair around, so I was beside her. "Tell me."

"It's not your problem," she said.

"Doesn't matter. Tell me."

Suzanne looked at me, and the tears started to form. "The bastard is suing me. For additional spousal support."

"Your... ex-husband?"

"Yeah," she said. "It's the primary reason I moved out of North Conway. The divorce was exceptionally messy; I caught him sleeping with his girlfriend *in our bed* and kicked his sorry ass to the curb. He proceeded to quit his six-figure job as an executive and pleaded poverty. My lawyer sucked, and I wound up barely getting out of there with my dignity."

"Ouch."

"Yeah. Now he's claiming that he should get more than what we agreed upon since I'm about to start my own practice. His lawyer reasons if I can afford to purchase both a book of business and a new building to house it..."

"Shit."

"My thoughts exactly," she said morosely. "They served me at the office this afternoon. I've been on and off the phone with lawyers ever since." She smiled as the waitress brought her another wine and put down my beer. "Fortunately, I left the state before I did anything rash like shoot him in the back."

I snapped upright and she caught my movement. "What?" she asked, perplexed.

"You... you have a gun?"

"Yeah," she smiled. "A nice one. A Glock of some sort, I couldn't tell you the exact model."

"Did you bring it here?"

"To the bar? No, silly," she said. The wine had affected her a bit and she seemed to be processing a bit slower than I would have expected.

"It's back at Charlie's." She saw my eyes widen and hastened to add. "Don't worry - she locked it up in her safe. The kids can't get to it."

"That's not what I was worried about," I said quietly.

"What?" Suzanne asked, still fuzzy around the edges.

"Nothing," I said, knowing that, in fact, everything had just gone to Hell. For Suzanne had just landed both her and Charlie on my list of suspects.

"How was your day?" Suzanne asked as she took a sip of her wine.

"Lousy," I said as I rubbed my now-aching temple. "And it keeps getting worse."

Twenty-Four

There was no point in calling out the troops and heading to Charlie's; I was already going to need to drop Suzanne off myself after dinner given how much wine she'd drunk at the bar, and I'd need an official warrant to open the gun safe, anyway. I'd barely touched my beer; in fact, I wasn't feeling very hungry at all, but still followed through with our plans for dinner. Surprisingly, Suzanne moved fairly well given how intoxicated she was, but just in case, I looped an arm through hers and walked side-by-side with her down the block or so to Millie's on the Wharf.

Aunt Mildred Martin - the Millie of the restaurant - was my mother's older sister and the spitting image of her. Her husband had passed years earlier, but that hadn't stopped her from continuing to run the second biggest tourist draw behind the Colonial. Charlie had tried to convince her mother to retire but Millie wouldn't hear of it; at sixty-eight, she was every bit as spry as the college-aged waitstaff always in her employ.

I pushed through the doors covered in plastic toy lobsters and walked the short hallway to the check-in counter. A student I didn't recognize was behind the podium, but she knew me. "Chief!" she smiled. "Nice costume last night."

I rolled my eyes. "It's out there, then?"

"Oh yeah," she laughed. "Detective Korsokovach is already seated."

"Perfect," I replied and tactfully propelled my tipsy companion around the corner and past the massive saltwater tank containing the lobsters that may well wind up on a patron's table that evening. We normally snared a Godfather-style circular booth in the far corner, and I spied Vasily and his date for the evening already engrossed in conversation.

I helped Suzanne take off her windbreaker and hooked it and my fleece over the coat hook. "Guys," I smiled as we slid into the booth.

"Chief," Vasily said. "I asked Mark to join us tonight to fill us in on his... calls," he said carefully. "I, uh, didn't know you'd have a guest."

"Yes," I said. "Maybe the three of us could step into banquet room briefly?" I suggested. "After we place our order? Suzanne can keep the table warm for us."

"Exactly!" she said brightly. "You go talk your police talk. I'll be right here."

I waved to the waiter who hurried over to us. "I'll take the Thursday Special," I said, "and one for my guest."

"Same for me," Vasily said. He looked pointedly at Mark.

"I'm... not staying," the young officer said. "Thanks anyway."

The waiter nodded and hurried back to the kitchen; the three of us made our way back toward the entrance but turned and entered the darkened banquet room. I flipped on one bank of fluorescents. "All right, go."

Vasily pulled out his notebook. "We found a gun safe under the bed in the master suite," he said. "It's at the station now, locksmith can't get to it until after eight." His eyes met mine. "Ammo was in the bookcase in her den."

"Lovely." I took a deep breath. "We have another to fetch, too."

"We do?" Vasily said, hand paused on his notebook.

"Yeah. Suzanne disclosed to me that she had a Glock when she moved to Windeport. It's locked up in Charlie's gun safe, apparently."

"Shit," Vasily said as he pulled out his phone. "I'll call the judge," he said, then turned to Mark. "Tell him what you dug up."

Mark looked at me and then down to his notebook. "I made it through the list of gun shops," he started. "Two are of interest. 'DeSalvo

Guns' in South China sold a Glock 17 to Yvette Bedard in 2012," he said. "The owner hastened to mention that Bedard was a frequent shopper, usually around hunting season; the Glock stood out for him as it was not something she'd use in the backwoods."

"No kidding," I said, trying hard to picture Bedard with *any* kind of gun.

"Second hit was 'Liberty Freedom' in Yarmouth. Menard LaChance purchased a Glock 17 - used, apparently - eight months ago."

"Eight months?"

"I asked twice," Mark smiled. "Oddly, he didn't buy any ammo; he just wanted the gun."

"That's... unusual. What do you do with a gun that has no ammo?"

"Mount it on the wall?" He flipped his notebook closed. "Should I follow up in person?"

"Yes," I said. "Get copies of any documents for the sales. It would be a bonus if they have signatures that we can match to IDs." I paused. "When you get back, invite both of the good Doctors to the station for an interview tomorrow evening."

His eyes bugged out. "Aren't you going to Boston tomorrow?"

"I am," I smiled. "They can wait for me to return on Saturday."

"I'll leave in the morning," he smiled. "Night, Chief."

Vasily wrapped his call a moment later and turned back to me. "I've got a verbal, and the hard copy will be in our inbox within the hour. How do you want to handle this?"

"Carefully," I said. "Very, very carefully."

Twenty-Five

My hunger hadn't returned, so dinner wound up being rather tedious. Suzanne was bubbly enough for the three of us, but my heart ached at what was about to happen. Technically, as a suspect, I had every right to redirect her to the station and the drunk tank. After sobering up, she *should* be subjected to a full interview. I looked at her, and the gentle smile that was still there even after all the wine and made a gut decision to screw protocol - and hope it didn't come back to bite me later.

I left Suzanne dozing in the SUV; Vasily and Lydia had gone on ahead of us, so I was the lucky one to face a storm-cloud-shrouded Charlie stomping around on her porch. Cautiously, I approached the bottom step. "Charlie," I nodded.

"You'd better have a damn good reason for invading my home, *cousin*," she said tightly. "You're *damn* lucky the kids are at a slumber party."

"I'm doing my job, *cousin*," I said as I stepped up to her level on the porch. "As unpleasant as this might seem, it's the only way I can do it correctly."

"Like Hell," she snorted. "What are you after, anyway?" she asked.

"It was on the warrant," I said, my eyes going to the crumpled paper at her feet.

Vasily appeared at the door to the house. "It's locked," he said simply.

I turned back to Charlie. "What's the code for the gun safe?"

Her eyes widened. "Why do you want to get into that old thing?" she asked. "It holds nothing but dust and bad memories." She was so earnest, she nearly had me convinced.

I nodded to Vasily who started to take notes again. "Did Suzanne ask you to store anything in that safe, Charlie?" I paused for a long moment. "Right now, it's just the two of us talking. Like family."

She stared at me.

"Please, Charlie," I said softly. "This is important. I don't want to have to go the paddy wagon route, but if I have to, I'll haul your ass to the station."

I'd known my cousin longer than anyone in town and recognized both the anger and fear in her eyes. Not fear of my threat - such as it was - but of something more. I nodded. "You know why I am here."

She nodded and stepped back. "The code is six-eight-three," she said to Vasily, who quickly relayed it to Lydia. Charlie then turned back to me with a half-smile. "It's the Dewey number for Household Appliances."

"When did she give it to you?"

Charlie sat on the edge of the railing. "Is this a formal interview, *Chief*?" she asked, emphasizing my title to make her point.

"It doesn't have to be. It's still just the two of us. Chatting in hypotheticals."

She looked at me for a long, long moment. "How much trouble are we in?"

"Honestly?"

"I'd expect nothing less."

I paused for a moment, knowing I was treading a line more closely than I should. "You're tangled up in a murder investigation now, Charlie. You probably shouldn't answer any of my questions, here on your porch - or anywhere, for that matter - without having some representation."

The color had drained out of my cousin's face. "Dear Lord."

"Think about it for a moment," I said. "Think *carefully*."

Vasily cleared his throat, and I turned toward him. He nodded slowly: they'd opened the safe and found what we'd come for. I turned back to Charlie, who had her hand pressed to her mouth and was looking at her stockinged feet.

"Charlie," I prodded gently. "Did Suzanne ask you to store her gun for her?"

She looked up at me, eyes wide; all traces of her anger were gone, replaced now by that fear I'd seen earlier. Most citizens took on that expression when they brushed up against the law; in my experience, it was generally the ones with *nothing* worth worrying about that wore it. "I'm placing my trust in you, Sean," she said.

"Charlie, you can't do that. I can't protect you; anything you say from this point forward--"

"Yes," she said simply. "Suzanne talked extensively about her ex, and how she'd purchased some protection against him."

"Protection," I echoed, eyes flicking to Vasily who had started to record the conversation on his iPhone. "What form did that take, exactly?"

"She'd seen the safe the night I took her in," Charlie continued. "The next day, she brought the gun in, asked to lock it up. Keep it safe, as it were." She looked at me, horrified. "The fact that she would even think she *needed* a gun to protect herself is unspeakable."

"Did you *take* the gun from her to put it into the safe?"

"No," she said. "She watched me open it and then placed it inside."

"You never touched it?" I asked.

"No."

I took a deep breath. "Charlie, what were you doing on Sunday?"

"Chores," she said without hesitation. "And prep work for the party. Why?"

"Did you leave the farm?"

"No -- yes, I had to get some milk, and went to the IGA."

My heart skipped a beat. "About when was that?"

"Lunch, or a little after."

"Anyone see you?"

The fear appeared again. "Sean, this sounds like you're trying to get an alibi out of me."

"Did anyone see you?" I asked again, pointedly. "At the store? On the street?"

"I'm sure someone did," she said. "It was Sunday after all."

"Okay," I said as Vasily exited the house. Lydia was behind him, carrying a brown paper bag. I looked back to Charlie. "I will need you to swing by the station tomorrow to sign an official statement. Can you do that before you go to the Library?"

"Yes," she said. Then, she asked again: "How much trouble are we in?"

I started down the steps and answered over my shoulder. "Enough," I said.

Twenty-Six

Against my better judgement, I left Suzanne in the care of Charlie after extracting a promise that she'd ensure Suzanne arrived at the station the following afternoon. I'd sent Lydia on to the station with the gun; after she cataloged it, we'd need to get it to the Crime Lab in Augusta to see if it matched the bullet we'd recovered. I was hoping she'd take that and whatever we found in Sylvia's lockbox directly there at first light.

Vasily rode with me back to the apartment; I'd decided we'd move up our timetable and head to Boston directly and deal with Jones so we could return and question our quartet of "persons of interest" in the afternoon. It didn't take long for the two of us to pack an overnight duffel, and then we were on the road once more, driving south into the beginnings of a snowstorm. For my part, I felt like it was a metaphor for the investigation as a whole.

As troubled as my thoughts were, I made for bad company. Vasily used my moody silence to pour over the documents we'd gotten from the Foundation; the rustle of paper was occasionally offset by his incessant tapping on his tablet.

"It's not professional of me to say this," I mused about an hour later. We'd just entered the Maine Turnpike and still had nearly three hours to go. The clock on the dashboard told me I'd need more coffee if I were to make it all the way in one piece.

"Say what?" Vasily asked.

I shot a glance and saw he'd pinned his hair up with a tablet stylus and had a second in his mouth. "Charlie was in town at the right time and had access to a gun that could have been used in the murder. I don't want the gun to match."

"She's family," he said as he kept reading. "I get it. But it would be a two-fer if it didn't match."

"I kind of want that, too," I said.

"I know." He paused as his phone beeped. "Lydia," he said. "The locksmith popped the safe; Glock 17."

"Damn."

"She says she'll leave for Augusta at six; lab opens at eight. Do you want her to wait?"

"Yes."

Vasily typed his reply. "Two guns now. Are you hoping for another when we interview Bedard and LaChance?"

"Or two," I laughed ruefully. "But I'll take just one match. I still need a *reason* though. Unless Pelletier had a substantial fine for overdue books, I can't see what motive Charlie had."

Vasily looked at me. "You *have* to bring her in," he said.

"There's no reason to," I insisted.

"We don't know that," he pointed out quietly. "You always say, 'we ask questions and keep asking questions until everything makes sense.' I think that's where we are right now: asking more questions."

"Shit," I replied.

"I know."

I sighed. "Text Mark. Have him pleasantly insist that Charlie stick around when she drops off Suzanne."

"Okay," he said and tapped away at his phone.

I left him to sift through the financials and focused on the road, stopping at the service plaza in Kennebunk to buy an overpriced extra-large cup of coffee. The further south we went, the more unsettled I was by the disjointed parts of the case; I felt as if the one thing tying all of it together was there, just out of reach. And the more I thought about it, the further it retreated.

Feeling like I needed a pick-me-up, I reversed myself and booked us back into the Ritz-Carlton. The clerk behind the desk was pleasant, despite it being nearly one in the morning when we arrived; his glance between myself and Vasily, though, spoke volumes as to how he viewed our relationship and why, perhaps, we were checking into the same room at that ungodly hour. I tried not to roll my eyes as I plucked the cardkeys from his hand and headed for the elevator. Such judgements in the new millennium were annoying at best, though given my current mood, it felt best to bite my tongue and let it go.

I managed to drop off to sleep quickly but woke up around three to see Vasily had the small light on next to his bed. I turned to see he was still up and seated cross-legged on his bed in a snug muscle t-shirt that emphasized his physique and (dear Lord) Chat Noir sleeping pants. He'd taken out his contacts and was peering at his tablet over the top of his round rimless glasses, intent on what he was reading.

"Dude," I said, squinting at the clock. "It's not a thriller you're reading over there. Get some sleep."

"You'd be surprised," he laughed as he turned to me. His hair was haphazardly in a bun, which on anyone other than Vasily would have looked terrible. "The accounting system they use at the Foundation is byzantine, but I think that is intentional. It's nearly impossible to track funds from when they enter the system to when they are disbursed."

"What?" I asked, snapping on my light, and leaning on an elbow.

"Yeah," he said. "It's actually quite clever, for it makes it possible to perform some pretty shady transactions that evade rules the State has about how monies can be spent."

I sat up completely. "Just a reminder: I'm a dumb jock. Keep the financials simple for me."

Vasily laughed. "We both know that's not true, but I'll simplify it a bit. I can draw nearly a straight line from Ingmar Pelletier to Ingmar Pelletier with this data."

I blinked. "That's about as clear as mud."

Exasperated, Vasily slid to the edge of his bed. "The money we're looking for - the double mortgages?"

I nodded.

"While the patron has been obfuscated by the system, I can see two donations that match the amounts Ingmar took out against his house. I've cross checked twice, and the dates line up. He took the loan and then two days later, the patron wrote a check to the Foundation." He paused. "Twice."

"Who got the funds?"

"Ingmar!" he cried. "It was tough to track, but all of the dollars wound up in the Extension accounts he controlled."

I nodded again, this time a bit slower. "I bet you are about to tell me they were then transferred to LaChance."

"Bingo," he said. "Barbara's records showed that much. Not all at once, of course; more in the beginning, and then over the last six months, in increasingly smaller amounts."

"Ah," I said. "Almost as if he'd grown suspicious. Does that match with his pulling of the data for the packet?"

"I can't tell yet," he said. "But I would bet so."

"Well done," I smiled.

Vasily smiled slightly at the compliment and considered me for a long moment before slowly setting his tablet down on the rumpled covers of his bed. As self-assured as he normally was, I was surprised to see him suddenly grow nervous, his brown eyes catching mine before dropping to consider his exposed shins. "Sean... I need to tell you something."

Growing more concerned, I tried to lighten the mood with some humor. "If it's about parking in my spot at the pharmacy, I've already told you—"

"*No*," he said fiercely as his head came up, shaking loose a long bang from his haphazard bun.

Shocked into silence, I let my half-smile fade. "Okay. What's up?"

Taking a deep breath, he then took another. "I... look, you know how much it means to me that you accept... who I am, right?"

I nodded. "From day one," I said slowly, wondering where he was going with this.

He looked away, that long lock of hair partially obscuring his face. "I think Deidre leaving you made me realize I finally needed to say something." Vasily turned back toward me, and I could see a slight tinge of color on his cheeks. "I..." he started, before swallowing, hard. "I've never said this to *anyone* before. Because no one has ever been *you*."

My eyes widened. "Vasily—"

"I love you, Sean," he blurted out in a rush of syllables. "I have from the moment I met you."

"You... *what?*" I breathed, my mind trying to comprehend what he'd just said.

"I love you," Vasily said more firmly, though his face started to flame deep crimson. It wasn't hard to see how difficult it was for him to verbalize what he was feeling. Squeezing his eyes shut, he took a deep breath again before plowing forward. "Can you... is it possible...?" he asked so softly I strained to hear him. He paused for a long moment before opening his eyes and looking at me directly, hopeful optimism in his eyes. "Do you... love me, too?"

All at once, I realized I'd completely missed the signals Vasily had been sending me, the looks, the comments, the casual touch here or there. I'd known him so long, I'd written them off as signs of our deep friendship, but now, as I looked into the face of the man I considered family, I saw it as something else entirely. My own actions, however inadvertent, seemed to have telegraphed an understanding that wasn't true; I found myself shaking my head, more in disbelief that I had managed to be so blind to what the two people closest to me had been feeling.

Vasily's face fell, partially misinterpreting my reaction. "Oh," he said heavily. "Crap."

"Vas—"

"I--look, I--" he spluttered, face impossibly turning a deeper shade of red as he turned away. "Damn. I'm sorry. I'm more tired than I realized."

"Vasily," I started, "that's a lot to take in—"

He turned back to me, eyes slick with emotion. "I know," he said softly, before quickly sliding all the materials on his bed into his hands and standing. "I'll finish this in the lobby," he added as he quickly fled the room, the door clicking shut behind him with a finality that cut me to the soul.

I sat there on my bed, wondering if I should follow him to the lobby. Vasily was my deepest, closest friend, but I simply wasn't built to give him what he genuinely wanted. And that realization cut me to the quick worse than anything I'd ever felt before.

Did I love him? I found myself wondering. *Yes,* I thought after a long moment. *But as the brother I never had.*

That was exactly what I had told him years earlier, though at the time it had garnered me a deep frown and a snort of disgust, but nothing more. I was certain now, sitting there on that bed, he had heard what he'd wanted to hear, and had kept his flame of desire lit, albeit on low.

All this time, I thought as a bolt of regret hit me, *I led him on without realizing it. He's my best friend! What the Hell have I done?*

Knowing sleep was not going to come easily now, I slid out of the bed and pulled my sweatshirt on, then stood at the window and partially opened the curtain. Looking back, I could make the case his string of failed relationships over the years could be tied to his unwavering faith that someday I would see the truth in his love; quixotically, the more I pushed away what I now realized had been his advances, the greater his belief we would soon turn a corner appeared to become.

I marveled to think at the *years* we had danced around the core issue, and somehow, it had not affected the friendship we shared, yet I knew Deidre's departure had been the final transit to a one-way fork in the road. And of the two options available, the *road closed* sign was still firmly in place on one.

"Shit," I said to myself. I grabbed the key to the room from the sideboard along with my iPhone and went in search of my partner and best friend.

The lobby was deserted when I arrived, which gave me pause. Slowly, I worked my way through the gilded room, aware that the night desk clerk had appeared, watching me while wearing a retail smile that reminded me I was not attired properly for the space as I padded around the slick marble barefoot. I caught his eye, smiled, then moved down a side hallway lined by potted plants with massive green fronds that led to the restaurant we had dined in before.

I found Vasily sitting on the rug, his back against one of the many pots holding a small date palm. Why hotels thought they brought something to the atmosphere was beyond me He had his knees pulled up to his chest, and had leaned his forehead into them; his hands were over his head as if he were fending off the world. The files he'd taken were scattered in front of him, clearly the result of him having thrown them against the far wall.

Silently, I sat down beside him and waited for a bit. My own thoughts were in turmoil, for the pain coming off Vasily in waves was palpable, and I was at a loss as to how to help him. I couldn't lie - there was no way I could love him as he wanted. But clearly, my friendship alone was no longer enough. Seeing him curled there on the floor crystalized that I had hurt him as much as Deidre.

What the Hell is wrong with you, Sean?

"Vasily," I said quietly. "I am truly sorry."

He sighed deeply. "It's not your fault," he said simply, twisting his head up slightly so I could see an eye. It was red-rimmed and bloodshot, making me feel even worse. "You've been honest with me from the beginning. That's more than most would provide me." He pressed his head down into his knees again. "I saw what I wanted to see. I am who I am, and I love who I love," he said very softly.

"And you love me," I said simply.

"From the day I met you," he repeated, and his voice caught.

"Vasily..."

"I know," he said, snuffling slightly. "I *know*."

"This feels a bit like I'm breaking up with someone," I said softly. "Doing it twice inside of a week tells me I suck at relationships." I sighed as I leaned back a bit. "I guess it's a bit like what you said. I am who I am, but it's not the guy you want."

"But you are," came the muffled response. "You are *exactly* the man

I want, and I thought I saw you felt the same. Holy hell," he snuffled again. "Over thirty and I still feel like a damn teenager with a crush."

"That's on me," I replied, a bit distraught. I tried to choose my next words carefully. "I do love you, but as a friend; no, more like I said years ago. Like family. I just... I can't love you the way you want me to."

"Family," Vasily snorted as he looked up at me, his hair sliding down into his face. "Lovely."

My breath caught, for even until that very moment I'd not fully appreciated the depth of his attraction to me. I tried to say something - anything, for that matter - but instead found myself sitting there, mouth slightly agape. Finally, I managed to gather myself.

"I... until just now, I'm not sure I understood." I placed my hand, carefully, on his shoulder. "I do now, and I am deeply, horribly sorry. I don't want to keep hurting you, as I clearly am."

"You're not," he said as he pushed his hair back behind an ear. "I'm doing it to myself. You've treated me with nothing but fairness, kindness, and respect. Whatever hurt I am experiencing is my own inability to look beyond the most perfect human being I've ever encountered." He smiled slightly. "It's not hyperbole - and I'm not just attracted to you physically. Your compassion for others is what initially endeared you to me - your loyalty to fairness, and equity in all that you do."

He looked to the wall. "Growing up as I did, it was easy to be cynical when people claimed to be open and affirming - and turned out to be anything but. You, my friend," he said turning back to me, "are the very definition. For me it's a powerful fragrance that's hard to ignore."

"Shit," I said. "That's... damn, Vasily. I'm afraid of the pedestal you've placed me on," I added. "If anything, this case has proven to me that I have some *serious* blind spots."

"We all do, Sean."

I looked at my friend, who had a look of deep longing on his face. "How do we move forward?" I asked softly, genuinely unsure. "What do you want to do? Want *me* to do?"

"Get you into my--"

"*Besides* that," I said, somewhat heartened that his good humor was peeking out.

He considered me. "I don't know," he said. "Honestly? I probably should get away from you - leave Windeport. Start over somewhere else and try to put you behind me." Vasily looked away. "I'm not sure I can do that; but then again, I'm not sure if I should stay, either."

"I think I understand," I said gently. "For the first time, maybe."

"I think you do too, now," he smiled. "And I am reasonably comfortable telling you I can't live without you in my life, even if it can only be as a friend."

"That's all I can offer, Vas," I replied softly. "You mean the world to me and have for a long time. But it won't go beyond the friendship we already enjoy."

"I know," he said, and I could see the sad realization finally settling in on his face. "I do."

I gripped his shoulder, a mute acknowledgement of everything and wondering if we'd really made any progress. Maybe, maybe not. Time would tell. "Come on," I said. "Let's get this stuff back to the room and grab what little shuteye we can."

"You go ahead," he said. "I need to sit here a bit longer." At the concern that crossed my face, he smiled thinly. "Don't worry, I left my gun upstairs."

"Vasily! That's not something to kid about!"

"Why do you think I left it in the room?" he chuckled at the wild expression I had to be wearing. "I'll be fine. I'll be up before we need to go to breakfast."

"Promise?"

"Promise."

Looking at him closely, I pushed myself up and stood. "Good," I said. "Because I'm not entirely sure what I would do if I ever lost you."

He nodded and smiled more warmly than he had in a bit. "Keep saying things like that..."

"Shit, Vasily," I laughed. "Just... shit."

Twenty-Seven

Vasily had eyes only for the waiter at breakfast, perhaps overcompensating in an effort to prove to me he was trying to get back to normal. I kept our conversation light, and my jokes lighter and before long we were out on the snow-covered sidewalks of Boston to surprise the editor at the *Journal* for our follow-up interview.

The storm we'd driven into had dominated the overnight hours, and the change to the city was amazing. Where just a few days before we'd had a faux late summer day, now we were bundled up against a squall that was depositing thick snowflakes across any and all surfaces. It was dark, gloomy, and uncomfortably chilly: all perfect representations of my frame of mind. I shot a glance at Vasily; he'd thought ahead enough to bring a knit cap to stuff his mane of hair into, though a shock of blond had escaped one edge.

Me, not so much. I tried to shrug off the snow that was accumulating on my shoulders and hunkered down against the strong wind swirling the snow around us. I couldn't be sure, but it felt like Boston had been caught off guard. The roads hadn't been plowed yet, and the sidewalks were slick and deadly. Traffic seemed pretty light, and I wondered if schools had been called out. Businesses seemed to be operating, given the lights we were passing in the various high rises, but foot traffic was rare.

This time around, Mike the watchdog was nowhere to be found as we pushed through the door to the suite for the *Journal*. I looked at

Vasily as we stood there in front of the empty reception desk, snow melting from our jackets and dropping to the floor.

"Hello?" I called out.

"Out back, come on in."

I picked my way to Jordan Small's office and found her shucking off her winter boots and stepping into a pair of running sneakers. "Lousy weather," she said as she looked up at me. "But not surprising. We always get nailed when we have a great fall day."

"Isn't that the truth," I smiled.

"What brings you back to my humble office, Chief?" Jordan said as she moved behind her desk and sat down. "Sit, please," she added belatedly, indicating the visitor chairs.

"We won't take much time," I said, halting Vasily who had started toward a chair. Ignoring his arched eyebrow, I continued. "I understand Ingmar Pelletier called you before he sent the packet to you."

"Did he?" she said.

"I don't have a lot of time," I said. "So, I'm going to cut to the chase here. He called you," I said, eyes flicking to Vasily and hoping he'd follow my lead.

He turned from me. "We have the phone records," he said. Which, of course, we didn't.

But she didn't have to know that. "What did the two of you discuss?" I asked.

Jordan looked at me, hard. "I don't know what you're asking," she said.

Looking at her carefully, I played a hunch. "Bedard's call afterward seems to have spooked you."

Jordan's eyes widened.

"I mean, you didn't even open the envelope, did you?" I waited a beat. "What did she promise you?"

Jordan stood and went to the coffee pot - a classic Mister Coffee if memory served - and poured herself a cup. As the pot didn't appear to actually be on, I was impressed at her lack of grimace when she sipped the day-old brew.

"What did she promise you?" I asked again.

Jordan sighed. "Membership on the Foundation Board," she said softly.

I raised my eyebrows. "That would seem to be a conflict of interest."

"Only if I were still the editor," she replied as she sat down again, coffee set aside, forgotten.

"So, you agreed to step down? And join the board? Why, exactly?"

She looked at me. "Do I--"

"Yes," I said shortly. "I need to hear it from you."

"Yvette Bedard asked me to bury the research and keep it from getting into the peer review process," Jordan said. "In return, I became the newest member of the Foundation. My resignation is effective next week."

"I hope you got her agreement in writing," Vasily said.

"I did," Jordan said, sliding open a drawer and retrieving an envelope. She tossed it at me. "You don't get as far in this industry as I do without covering your bases."

Taking the envelope, I flipped it over to see it was a logoed envelope from the University. Opening it, I retrieved a letter from the Foundation formalizing Jordan's appointment to the board. I tried not to choke at the salary attached to what I'd assumed was more of an honorary post; no wonder their financial system was so byzantine. I looked to Vasily. "I'd like a copy, if I could."

"Take it," she smiled. "I have one already."

"Thank you," I said, and we turned to leave the office.

Out in the hallway, while we waited for the elevator, Vasily looked at me. "How did you know about Bedard's call?" he asked.

"I didn't," I said. "But I know Bedard. Call it a lucky guess."

We hiked back to the hotel; Vasily looked longingly at a Starbucks we passed along the way, but for some reason I was ready to get back to Windeport. Not long after, we'd checked out of the hotel and started the long slog northward through the inclement weather.

I couldn't help but feel like the storm was following us.

Twenty-Eight

Snowplows *were* out in Windeport when we drove across the town line on Route One; the drive from Boston had been slow, and in some parts, had seemed almost like driving through molasses - even in an SUV. The accumulation was impressive for a storm all the weather forecasters had predicted would be a fast-mover and limited. Once more, we'd been promised a good weekend only to have it become a bona fide Nor'easter at nearly the last minute.

Vasily had taken the wheel after I'd finally relented and found a Dunkin' Donuts just outside of Portsmouth. After flipping positions, I'd grabbed his tablet and started to review the case file again, prepping for what I knew would be exceedingly difficult interviews with both friends and family. Bedard, of course, was firmly on the enemy list, but that was neither here nor there.

It wasn't lost on me how little conversation the two of us had over the journey home.

By the time we pulled into the station, I had a sense of how I wanted to proceed and what I was hoping to find out. The surprise would come, perhaps, with which person revealed the one piece of the puzzle I was still missing.

Caitlyn was at Reception when we entered the lobby, and smiled when I came in. "Chief," she said. "Nice weather we're having. Public Works sent over the street closures," she said, handing me a manilla folder.

I saw the seal from the village and flipped it open. "They could have emailed it," I laughed.

"Not their way," she chuckled. "Also, Lydia called in. She's stuck in Augusta, literally; the Crime Lab is snowed in. They've got cots and everything."

"Seriously?" I said, looking out the window and seeing maybe a foot of accumulation. "That's nothing," I laughed, waving at the snow.

"They have nearly twenty inches inland," she said. "It's been snowing since midnight."

"Yikes. Please tell me she got my lab results, though…?"

"No such luck, Chief. The tech didn't make it in."

I looked to Vasily. "This will make things interesting."

"Yes."

I turned back to Caitlyn. "Well, get everyone on standby, then. Looks like it's gonna be a long night."

"Overtime!" she said happily as she started dialing a number on the phone. "And just in time for the Christmas holiday, too."

"There goes my carefully crafted budget," I muttered as we badged into the rear and walked into the bullpen area. Most of my limited staff were already out and about helping our sibling departments prepare and/or deal with the storm, so it was quiet save for the lone officer standing in front of the four interview rooms at the far end of the space. From the lit windows in at least two, I knew our guests were here and cooling their heels.

I nodded to George, who was ex-Marine and technically a retiree of the department. He worked a few days a week to qualify for medical benefits until he passed over the line for Medicare. Vasily followed me into my office where I shed my jacket and made a beeline for the Keurig.

"Seriously?" Vasily said, and I turned to see an arched eyebrow.

"We only made the one stop," I said defensively. "And I'm going to need this."

He nodded. "Who's on first?"

"No," I said, "he's on second."

Rolling his eyes, he just turned and led me back across the cubicle farm to the interview rooms. "You want me on the mirror? Or in the room?"

I thought about that. "Protocol would be one-and-one," I sighed. "Screw it," I muttered as I randomly picked the first door and entered.

Suzanne looked up from the table, and Charlie was sitting across from her. "Sean?" she asked, her eyes wide. "What's going on? We've been here for hours."

"I know," I said, "and I'm sorry. I was detained, and the snow made travel worse."

"This is not acceptable at all, *Chief*," Charlie said icily. "I dropped her off as you asked, and then was told I couldn't leave." She held up her hands, which still bore the ghost of fingerprint ink. "We're being treated like criminals."

"I know," I repeated. "I'm the one who asked the officers to keep you here." I looked to Vasily. "Would you make sure that Charlie gets a cup of coffee? And then put her in Number Two."

"I don't need coffee," she said. "What I need is an explanation."

"You'll get it," I replied. "I'll be in shortly."

Vasily nodded and escorted Charlie out; I stood against the door, keeping it open to the cubicle farm until Vasily returned and we both took seats across from Suzanne. The interview room was done up in typically get-on-your-nerves style: stark white walls, one-way mirror on one wall, overly loud ticking clock on the other. The only nod to modernity was the switch under the table that I used to activate the recording system.

"This is Chief of Police Sean Colbeth with Detective Vasily Korsokovach," I started, then added the date and time. Turning to Suzanne, I asked: "Please state your name and current address."

"Suzanne Kellerman," she said, eyes wider than I thought was humanly possible. "I'm currently residing at two-oh-seven Dairy Farm Road."

"Miss Kellerman— "

"Mrs. Kellerman," she corrected. "Technically. The divorce is being contested."

I tried not to let the shock show on my face. "Mrs. Kellerman, I need to formally inform you of your rights before we go much further." I looked to Vasily, who recited from memory the Miranda Warning.

Sliding our standard Miranda Release form toward her, he asked: "Do you understand these rights?"

Suzanne looked at me, fear clear on her face. "Am in trouble? *Serious* trouble?"

"I don't know, honestly," I said. "But you are well within your rights to ask for a lawyer. However, you can suspend that right and talk to us -- to me," I nearly pleaded, "if you sign that form."

"But be very sure that is what you want," Vasily said unexpectedly.

I shot a glance at him. "Exactly," I said carefully as I turned back to Suzanne.

She looked at me. "I trust you, Sean," she said slowly. "I'll tell you what you want to know, whatever that is," she finished, taking the paper, and signing the waiver.

After making sure the form was duly noted for the record, I turned back to her. "Suzanne, tell me about your gun."

"What about it?" she replied. "There's not much to tell. I bought it after I separated from my ex," she said. "He was... physically abusive for most of the time I was married to him, and he has repeatedly threatened to kill me for leaving him."

I blinked. "And he's suing *you* for spousal support?"

"I know, right?" she laughed humorlessly. "He had a cozy corner office that he left so he could stick it to me one more time."

"And how long have you owned it?"

"Two years," she said.

"Do you have the purchase record with you, here in Windeport?"

"Maybe," she said, thinking. "It's probably in my important papers, but I've not unpacked yet."

I looked at Vasily. "It might be helpful if you can dig it out. Or tell us where you bought it."

"Why?" she asked.

"Reputable dealers will record the serial number at time of purchase," Vasily explained. "Seeing your receipt or talking to the dealer will let us confirm ownership of the gun we retrieved from Charlie's safe."

"Oh," she said. "That makes sense. It might be faster to talk to the dealer, then. Frampton Hunting Supplies, in North Conway."

Vasily looked at me, then back to her. "We'll call them and confirm, if we have your permission?"

"Absolutely," she said.

"Tell me again how the gun came to be in Charlie's safe?" I asked.

Suzanne groaned. "If you are hoping to catch me in a lie, I have only a vague recollection of what we talked about at dinner."

I smiled, somewhat genuinely. "Go ahead."

"Well, you already know that I was trying to book a room at the Colonial until my apartment is ready," she started, fixing her eyes on mine. "Since I am being held up by the current tenant, that was my only option."

I nodded.

"I happened to mention that to Charlie while I was at the Library shortly after I arrived, and she insisted I stay with her. I accepted her offer. I was up front with her about the gun; the night I arrived, she took it from me and put it in the safe." She shrugged. "I've not seen it since."

"Charlie *took* the gun from you?"

"Yes."

"Can you tell me your movements from eight a.m. on Saturday to eight a.m. Monday?"

"That's easy," she said. "I was in Bangor overnight. With the hours of the practice I'm taking over, I had to make a special appointment to visit with the company that will be handling our EMR system and hardware."

"EMR?" I asked.

"Electronic Medical Records," she translated. "The current system is DOA, so we need a new one and equipment to run it."

"Computers? Tablets?"

"Yeah."

"When did you get back to Windeport?"

"Late-afternoon Sunday? I was at dinner with Charlie and her kids."

"What is your relationship to Ingmar Pelletier?"

"The dead professor?"

"Yes."

"None, as far as I know. I've never lived in this part of the state before."

"No family in the area?"

"I don't have a secret sibling, Chief," she laughed. "Sorry."

"Did you hear or see anything even remotely unusual during that period? Or in the days leading up to the weekend?"

"No?" she said. "I mean, I've not lived in this town very long, so I'm not sure I know what is 'normal' yet at this point."

I smiled. "All right," I said.

"That's it?"

"For now. Hang tight for a bit longer if you don't mind."

"Okay," she said slowly. "Can I at least get some coffee?"

"Yes," I said. "Come on, you can use my Keurig."

Vasily started to say something and I silenced him with a glare. "Go sit with Charlie," I said firmly. "I'll be in shortly."

"Okay, Chief," he said, but I knew he was not impressed with me.

Suzanne followed me into my office, and I offered her a clean mug and her choice of K-Cups. "Be honest, Sean," she asked me softly. "How serious is this? Was it my gun--"

"I can't tell you that," I said quickly, my eyes darting to the door. "But is important that you tell me *everything*. Absolutely everything."

"I did!" she said as she pulled the mug out from the Keurig.

"Are you sure, absolutely sure, there was nothing strange or out of the ordinary last weekend?"

"Pretty sure," she said. "I mean, I did have to detour to Augusta for Charlie, but it wasn't that far out of the way."

I kept my face impassive. "Really? Why?"

"She said she needed some fabric from Michael's so she could finish your costume. She'd called around and the one over by that ugly Civic

Center was the closest branch that had that spandex in stock." Her mouth quirked as she added, "I think it was time well spent, purrsonally."

Trying to stay in investigator mode while simultaneously knowing she was picturing me in my costume was a Herculean challenge, but I managed to come through it. "How late did that make you?"

"Late enough that dinner was in the oven when I got back. But not so late that I couldn't join her and the kids at the table."

"So, what, around five?"

"Sounds right."

"Okay," I smiled. "Do you mind waiting here?"

"Instead of that tiny room? Are you kidding?"

"Good," I said, feeling marginally better. "Then I'll *catch* you in a bit," I punned as I left her behind.

Vasily was leaning against the door jamb as I exited, turning off his iPhone's recording function. "That was a bit of a gambit," he said quietly as we moved toward the interview rooms again.

"I thought if she were more comfortable with a cup of coffee, I might get something."

He nodded appreciatively. "Now what?" he asked. "For she essentially threw your cousin under the bus."

"I know," I said grimly as I put my hand on the door. "And I want to know why."

Twenty-Nine

The temperature went down twenty degrees when we entered the room. Yvette Bedard was sitting with her back against the wall in a tasteful professional pantsuit, which was completely offset by the scowl she fixed on us as we sat down across from her. Repeating the same process we'd performed with Suzanne, Bedard predictably signed the waiver and then started shouting at us.

Once she ran out of air, I started in. "Do you own a gun, Professor?"

"That would be 'Doctor,'" she corrected darkly. "And yes, I own multiple guns."

"Do you own a Glock, *Doctor*?" Vasily asked.

"Yes," she nodded.

"Where did you purchase that particular gun?"

"DeSalvo, in South China," she said curtly.

Wanting to catch her off guard, I asked: "When did you start having sex with Ingmar Pelletier?"

Bedard's eyes widened, and she started laughing, that same watery-choking noise I'd heard before. "Sex? With that old cow?"

"Yes."

"You are not a very good investigator, Chief, if you believe whatever you think you know about me and Doctor Pelletier," she laughed.

"You weren't in a relationship with Pelletier?"

"No," she laughed again. "Well, maybe," she corrected. "A *business* relationship."

Suddenly, a different reason for the run in that Michael had witnessed in the tunnels below campus sprung to mind. "One that soured recently, I suspect."

"That much is true," she said. "The idiot was about to ruin us."

"After pouring so much money into the project," I nodded.

"Yes," she said. "About six million, total. But we had two companies lined up to license the work; he had to go and read one paper too many, that old fool."

I did some math in my head and realized it was likely that Pelletier had poured a third of the total dollars into the project from his own personal sources. "How were the fees to be split?"

She looked at me, wondering if I was confirming information or gathering it. "Our agreement would have covered what he'd put into it himself, and a small amount above that to manage the licenses on an annual basis. The University got the rest."

"Except he sent the packet to the *Journal*."

"I made sure it was spiked."

I nodded. "When did you find out the research was flawed?"

"Is it?" she asked me. "It's a matter of interpretation, don't you think?"

"Then why prevent it from being peer-reviewed?"

She looked at me again. "We were about to sign the license agreements. There had been rumors that the research was not totally solid, unfounded rumors mind you, so it was in the best interests of all to lock down the investment to keep going."

I nodded again. "So, you called the editor at the *Journal*."

"Yes."

"But that wasn't the end," I said, thinking I knew what Pelletier had done.

"No," she said angrily. "That fool called two of the four companies and told them about the article, and that there were issues. One of them - our largest investor - came to the conference specifically to discuss it with him."

"Lucky for you, he was unavailable," Vasily said.

"I didn't kill him," she said tartly.

"Where is your gun now?" I asked.

"In my glovebox. I presumed you'd not allow me to bring it into the station, otherwise it would be in my purse."

"You keep it on you at all times?"

"Yes."

"And where were you between eight on Saturday morning and eight on Monday morning?"

Bedard narrowed her eyes. "I took a suite at the Colonial, Chief. I have receipts and two hundred people who saw me; I was wining and dining every high roller I could get my hands on."

"I can believe that," Vasily said.

I shot him a look but didn't disagree, then turned to Bedard again. "I'm going to need your gun, Doctor," I said. "I'll have the officer outside help you retrieve it."

"Fine," she said. "Am I free to go?"

"For now," I said, and admittedly, liked the flare of fear that appeared briefly on her face.

Standing, I opened the door and told George what to do, then turned to Bedard. "Thank you for your time, Doctor."

"Like Hell," she said as she stormed out.

I waited until she was out of earshot before observing, "She could have slipped away from the hotel at any point in our window and not have been missed. We're going to have to track that story down."

"Just like Suzanne," Vasily added pointedly.

"Just like Suzanne."

Thirty

Charlie was next up and probably the interview I was looking forward to the least; actually, that was saying something, considering Yvette Bedard had been in the mix. Sighing with resignation, I started toward Interview Two; just as I put my hand to the doorknob, the lights in the station flickered and went out.

"That's not a sign or anything, is it?" Vasily laughed as we stood there in the semi-darkness of the mid-afternoon.

"No," I replied. "Let's go see how bad this is."

"You're just avoiding your cousin," Vasily needled.

"With good reason," I said as we worked our way to the lobby under the sparse emergency lighting.

Caitlyn was just getting off the phone as we came through the door. "Snowplow on Route Thirty-Five took out three poles close to the substation," she said. "Driver hit a patch of ice on that nasty curve outside of Springfield; he's fine, but the truck is toast. As are our chances of getting power back anytime soon."

"Ah," I said. "So, it's not just Windeport."

"No," she nodded. "About half the county is fed from that main."

"Lovely," I said.

"Phil went to check on the generator," she added before I could ask why our lights hadn't come back. "He grumbled about the maintenance budget being cut on his way out the door."

"I feel like a lecture is coming on," I said. "Internet?"

"Out, too. The plow made short work of that as well. Our phones are routed along Route One, though," she reminded me, "on the E-911 cables, but the rest of the town might not be as lucky."

I looked to Vasily. "Had we sent over the fingerprints to the lab?"

"No," he said. "But since they were closed..."

"Good point." I sighed. "Best case now is that we don't get anything until Monday."

"Likely," he said.

Mark chose that moment to come through the door, allowing a cold gust of wind to carry a quantifiable amount of snow in behind him. It took some effort for him to close the door. "Chief," he nodded as he stomped the snow from his uniform boots. "I'm glad I caught you. I did some digging this morning and found courtesy of the Feds that Sylvia's father is living in Sarasota and having his Social Security direct deposited to a local credit union there."

"Nice," I said.

"I made some calls and connected with a LEO that offered to do a wellness check. They just called back - father gave up the fact that his daughter had come to visit but had stepped out for groceries. It was apparently unexpected." He frowned at the last part. "Cell service cut out before I got anything else."

"Lines are down," I said. "You might be able to use Caitlyn's 911 trunk though, just don't tie it up long."

"What do you want them to do?" he asked.

I considered that. "Tell them... she's a person of interest in an open case for us, and we need to speak with her. It would be a welcome favor if they could locate her and make her available for questioning."

"On it," he said as he trotted to the back office.

I looked at Vasily. "I wonder what the family emergency was," I said. "But if she were fleeing, going to family is not the best move; she'd have to know that would be among the first places we'd check."

"I feel like a trip to the Sunshine State is in our future," Vasily replied. "The white sands of Sarasota are nice this time of year."

"Of *course* you would know that," I said, rolling my eyes. "Come on, let's chat with Charlie and then see if we need to go after Sylvia."

On our way back to the interview room, I went via my office to make sure Suzanne was still comfortable, then joined Vasily inside Two. The tiny rooms were inhospitable in the best of times; under the weak emergency lighting, it felt as though we were in an unbelievably bad science fiction end-of-days movie.

"Sorry to make you wait," I said as we sat down.

Charlie just stared at me for a long moment.

Steepling my fingers, I leaned back in my chair only to have the fluorescents burst into life. That made me smile. "Phil worked his magic," I said.

"Good." This came from Charlie. "It was actually getting quite cold in here."

I nodded, for in just the limited time the power had been off, my fingers had gone numb. Once more, I triggered the recording system and introduced everyone for the tape, then had Charlie provide her name and full address for the record.

Vasily recited the Miranda Warning from memory and I slid the paperwork toward her. Before I even had a chance to explain it to her, Charlie had taken the pen and signed the waiver, then tossed the pen down defiantly. "Go on, then."

Taking a deep breath, I plowed straight in. "Am I going to find your fingerprints on Suzanne's gun?"

Whatever she had been prepared to say to me, she'd apparently not anticipated that particular question. "I..." she started.

"Charlie," I said very deliberately. "Please think carefully before responding."

My cousin seemed to deflate slightly. Looking at her hands, she said softly, "Yes."

"Why? Why will I find them?"

Charlie shifted in her chair.

"Charlie?" I prompted, though part of me really didn't want to hear anything more.

"Fine." She looked back at me. "*Fine.*" Shifting, she looked at the mirror, then the clock, sighed deeply, and then caught my eye again. "I was going to kill Yvette Bedard with it."

"Charlie," I said, trying to hide my shock. "You're admitting to--"

"Like Hell," she said. "I didn't go through with it, did I? The old goat was just here."

"Maybe some context would help, then," Vasily said.

"The gun went into my safe pretty much the way I described it, but maybe not exactly," she continued. "It might have been the second day she was with us; I took her to the den, and she handed it to me to put it in the safe."

I nodded.

"As I was opening it, though, I realized I had an opportunity." She looked up at me. "I lied to you earlier - the safe is full of David's guns still. When David passed, I just wasn't able to part with them. Hunting had been such a part of his life."

"I remember."

"Anyway, as I put her gun in, I saw his, and it made me angry all over again."

I looked to Vasily. "Why?"

"Bedard fired David a month before we got the cancer diagnosis," she said. "He was one of two liaisons to the Extension." Laughing coldly, she continued. "She'd said it was just business, that the budget couldn't support both Pelletier and my husband. I think it had more to do with the fact that Ingmar seemed able to bring in magic dollars that David wasn't."

I nodded again. "It doesn't appear to have been all that magical."

"Really?" She laughed ruefully. "Well, it doesn't matter now, but I'm still convinced losing his job hastened his death. Thank goodness we had decent life insurance; I nearly lost the farm."

"Go on."

"Well, Suzanne told me she had to go to Bangor and it just suddenly popped into my head. I took the kids to Mom's--"

"Millie?"

"Yes. Then I went back to the farm, got the gun, and drove up to the Colonial. I'm not sure I knew exactly what I wanted to do, but as I pulled up, I saw her waiting at the entrance. Before I could do anything, the valet pulled around me with her car and she was off."

"You followed her," I said.

"Yes. And damn it if she didn't drive over to Pelletier's house!"

"Did you confront them?"

"No. They were standing in the front driveway, such as it is; Pelletier looked like a homeless man in a stained t-shirt and totally inappropriate shorts. Bedard was dressed to the nines." She laughed. "They were already going at it; both seemed quite angry, enough that they didn't see me pull up."

"No kidding," I said. "Then again, Bedard *is* a force of nature."

"That is true." Charlie put a stray hair back in place. "Oh, dammit Sean, it was a stupid idea, and I knew it the moment I put the car into park. Bedard did turn and saw me but kept right on chewing out old Pelletier. Didn't even miss a beat."

"You never got out of the car?" I asked pointedly.

"No."

"How long did you stay out front?"

"Three minutes, maybe." She laughed ruefully again. "I'm not particularly good at this whole cold-blooded murder thing. I put my car into drive and pulled out; I hit the grocery store to pick up some milk and then went home."

"Did you call Suzanne?"

"Yeah," she said, and for the first time she flushed a bit. "I sent her on a fool's errand. I realized my Ring doorbell had caught my coming and going and needed time to figure out how to delete the record from the cloud. It required a lengthy phone call to tech support, and I didn't need someone to overhear it."

"Ring?" I echoed, turning to Vasily.

"It's one of those new-fangled video doorbells," Charlie explained. "Let's me watch for deliveries while I'm still at the library." She paused. "You've at least seen the ads for them, right?"

"No," I said.

"Jesus. Half the people in Windeport have them."

My head snapped to Vasily. "Do they?"

"I'll check," Vasily said, answering my unspoken question.

"I'm sorry, Sean," Charlie said. "I should have told you earlier. I realize this makes me look bad."

"It does," I said.

"What now?" she asked.

"Pray," I advised, "for we are still waiting on the gun tests."

"Shit."

Thirty-One

"This whole thing is nutty," Suzanne said as she gingerly sipped on the glass of red I had poured her. Mindful of our last encounter, she'd been nursing her first glass for more than an hour.

We were sitting in my apartment and it was close to seven; I'd released both her and Charlie, but Charlie had decided the roads were too bad to risk driving back to her farm. The twins were already at Millie's, so she drove the short distance there. I'd offered the spare room we had to Suzanne and to my surprise she'd said yes before I'd finished the sentence.

"It is," I allowed.

"Am I still a suspect?"

"Technically, yes, but I am pretty confident that we have enough to clear you," I said, omitting the aspect of her gun possibly being matched as the murder weapon.

The pharmacy had often stored perishable merchandise and still had a working generator; fortuitously, I'd thought to have the propane tank topped off a few weeks earlier. Still, the apartment didn't have more than the furnace and one or two overhead lights that were operational. Vasily had resorted to cooking over the Sterno stoves we had for emergencies, which meant our tomato soup and grilled cheese sandwiches were taking a lot longer than normal.

I looked at my darkened Keurig and tried not to mewl. Instead, I sipped my Sam Adams. "We're probably going to have to go to Florida tomorrow or Sunday," I said quietly, "but are you free for dinner on Tuesday?"

"I am," she said. "But I'm cancelling if you arrest me."

"Deal."

After eating our repast, Suzanne retired to her room and Vasily and I sat over a wide candle on the kitchen's breakfast bar. Keeping my voice low so she wouldn't hear us discussing the case, I asked: "If any of those houses along Ocean View Avenue have that Ring-thingy, might it have captured something around the time of the murder?"

"Yes," he said as he sipped a whisky on the rocks. "Are you buying Charlie's story?"

"No reason not to," I said. "But I need outside proof. Either way."

He nodded. "We can check on Suzanne's alibi once everything goes back to normal on Monday." Vasily paused as he downed the last of his whisky and then poured himself another slug. "But it all goes to Hell if the gun comes back as a match."

"I know. But I don't think it will."

Vasily looked at me, and despite the fact it was his fourth or fifth glass (I'd lost track), he didn't seem tipsy in the least. "That leaves Bedard or Gauthier. Who do you like for this, then?"

"Gauthier ran," I ticked off on my finger, "long before we knew she was a suspect. That's problematic, but she didn't run *away*. She ran *to* the relative safety of her parents."

"Pun intended," he smiled.

"Yeah. And her willingness to meet with us when we get down there is also not exactly in line with being the murderer," I added, alluding to the fact that Mark had actually managed to make direct contact with her via the Sarasota contact.

"And Bedard?"

I ticked the second finger. "We now have a witness that puts her at Pelletier's house on the afternoon of the murder."

"But Charlie admits to being there, too," he pointed out.

"Exactly. I need *something* to clarify all of this," I groaned, pressing my hands to my eyes.

"There's no one else? No out-of-the-blue suspect we've overlooked?"

I put my hands on the table. "That only happens on television," I said darkly. "This isn't *Law and Order*."

"Says the guy who claims not to watch it. Duly noted nonetheless," he laughed. "I'll book us on the next flight I can get. First Class okay?"

"Like Hell," I retorted as I stood and headed down the hallway.

"Sean," Vasily said as he quickly caught up to me. "One thing."

I turned.

"Don't we need to start packing?" he asked. "I mean, it's not long until the fifteenth…"

"Probably should," I said. "We can deal with it when we get back from Florida, I suppose."

"All right," he replied. "I'll email you the flights once I have them booked."

"Sounds good."

Thirty-Two

Vasily managed to book us on a late-morning flight out of Portland into Tampa via Atlanta, though I grimaced at the price tag that had come with the last minute ticket; we arrived at the modern airport to low seventies and heavy humidity as we retrieved our rental car from the garage. I thought it best not to complain, considering the power had yet to be restored as we'd left Windeport that morning - and it had started to snow again, the back half of a weather pattern that was flummoxing the television meteorologists.

Along with the power, the cable company was now telling us it could be a week or more before the lines were repaired that connected us to the internet; I decided to send Mark to the Crime Lab with the fingerprint cards we'd taken from everyone at their interviews. We had to get Bedard's gun there anyway, so with luck, by the time we returned we might have a slew of results to plow through.

Navigating out of the airport proved more complicated and time consuming than I'd anticipated; I found myself wondering if the inordinate number of retirees in the area had spontaneously decided to clog the major thoroughfares of the city, given it was Sunday. Vasily's iPhone had initially told us it would be a little more than an hour to get there, but an accident on I-275 proved it to be a poor choice, tacking on another hour to the entire affair. By the time we pulled into the small lot behind the palm-tree-shaded municipal building in Sarasota, my temper was short and my patience shorter.

"This is why I'll never move here," I grumbled as I turned off the car and took some deep breaths to try and clear my mind.

"Here," Vasily said, pulling something out of his backpack and handing to me.

"What the Hell is this?" I said, turning the small can around in my hands and seeing the Starbucks logo.

"One of those new espresso shot drinks. I figured you'd need an infusion of caffeine by now and picked up some while you were getting the car."

I popped the top and took a sip. "Oh wow," I said as I sat back against the headrest and closed my eyes in appreciation. "I *did* need that." Cracking an eye open, I smiled at Vasily. "I should be worried that you know me that well."

"Maybe."

I laughed and drained the can, feeling the elixir of life flowing into my veins. "All right, let's get this over with."

Vasily's contact - Detective Larry Halloran - was waiting for us at the main lobby desk. I tried not to stare, for the well-appointed space was four times as large as ours in Windeport and staffed accordingly. "Vasily?" the stout, balding man asked as he held out his hand.

"Larry!" Vasily said, pumping the older man's arm. "Good to put a face to the voice. This is my boss, Chief Sean Colbeth."

"A pleasure, sir," I smiled as I took his hand. "You've saved us a ton of time. I owe you big time."

"Send down some Lobster and we'll call it even," he laughed.

"I can do that," I said. "Fresh or just the meat?"

"Oh, fresh," he said. "I grew up on Nantucket, and the stuff they pull out of the Gulf and *call* lobster down here is a crime all by itself." He started walking toward a set of doors. "Ms. Gauthier is in our lounge -- that's what we call one of the interrogation rooms," he added as an aside. "It's wired for audio and video, so everything will be captured."

"Have you Mirandized her?" I asked.

"Yes, but she's also waived her lawyer," Larry said as he paused to badge open the door with his ID. "It's a bit of a grey area for us. Technically, in Florida she's not committed any crimes that we know of. She's here to assist you in an investigation; are you charging her with a crime? In Maine?"

"I'm not sure yet," I said honestly. "There is conflicting evidence, but she is tangentially connected in some way."

"Our laws would respect an outstanding warrant, but you'd need to make a more formal request for arrest and extradition." He sighed. "It's possible that any questioning you do here might not be admissible in Maine. I can recall one other case like this - a guy on the run from Texas, in that one -- and he confessed to several counts of fraud only to have it tossed out in Texas."

"We'll keep it in mind," I said.

Larry took us through to the main portion of the station, down a side corridor and into what for all the world looked like a standard break room. Sylvia was leaning on the counter with a cup of coffee; for a woman who may have committed murder, she appeared quite ordinary. "I'll leave you to it," Larry said as he closed the door behind us.

"Sylvia," I said as I moved to the old-style coffee maker and poured a fresh mug; I caught Vasily's shocked look, knowing as he did how I'd downed the espresso in the rental car. "You are a hard woman to locate."

"Sorry," she said out of the gate. "I just had to get out of there."

"Why?" I asked. "Your boss at the Colonial told us it was a family emergency."

She rolled her eyes. "In a way, I suppose."

"I have to admit, when we spoke the morning of Pelletier's death, I had the distinct impression you were not terribly enthusiastic to spend time with your parents. And yet," I waved my hands at the general area, indicating Sarasota, "here you are."

"A bit of hyperbole on my part. And not altogether wrong; having them with me in the bungalow in Windeport is a pain in the ass. I wind up being their maid, chauffeur, and chef."

"Why are you here in Sarasota, then?"

Sylvia looked at me. "Did you know that Maine is only one of a handful of states to pass the Death with Dignity act?"

"I am well aware of that fact."

"Ingmar Pelletier was dying," she said, "and all of us left on his street knew it."

"Cancer," I nodded. "We found it during the autopsy."

"Yeah. He had a few months left according to that quack of a doctor he had. But being the uptight moral ass he was, Doctor Philbert was refusing to go along with his wishes to end it all early."

My eyes opened a bit wider. "He wanted to end his life? Using the new law?"

"Yes." She looked away. "I wasn't particularly close to Ingmar, but he was a neighbor. So, for the last few months, I'd been helping when I can - getting him to appointments, shopping for groceries and the like. I even drove him to see that new doctor that is replacing Philbert - what's her name...?"

"Doctor Kellerman," I said, ignoring Vasily's pointed look at me.

"Right. I took him up at the end of the week and waited for him - he'd hoped the new doc would agree to his request."

"Did she?"

"Yes," she said, "but she warned him that her Medical License hadn't fully transferred over to the State yet, so she'd have to convince Philbert to go along with it in order to prescribe the medicine for him. Still, it was the most hope he'd had in months..."

Sylvia looked at me, and then away again. "Enough hope, in fact, that he called me over that Saturday to return my gun."

"Your gun," I said slowly.

"Yeah," she replied quietly.

"He... was considering alternatives, shall we say?"

She looked up, her eyes moist. "He was in an awful place, Chief, with no relief in sight. A few weeks ago, he was convinced that he would never be able to change Philbert's mind, and he wasn't feeling strong enough to venture to a new doctor and start the whole process over again. I was dropping off his groceries on a random weeknight when he lamented how he wanted it to all go away; how he'd wished he'd kept one of his old hunting rifles."

Sylvia heaved a deep sigh. "He asked me - dear God, he had to beg really - for me to get him a gun. I refused at first, but over the next few days I broke down. I have a Glock; I brought it to him and promised to look the other way."

"He returned it to you, you said?"

"Yeah. Saturday."

"Day before he died," Vasily pointed out. "From a gunshot wound."

Sylvia blanched.

"From what we suspect very strongly was a Glock," I added. "So, you can see why we are more than a little interested in why you are here and not in Windeport."

She looked between us and then to the ceiling, swore, and pulled out a pack of Marlboros.

"I don't think--" Vasily started before I waved him off.

Sylvia shook out a cigarette and lit up; a moment later, she'd exhaled a small halo of smoke, closing her eyes in bliss. "When I found him on Monday, I was shocked to see that he'd gone back to his original plan. I knew it couldn't have been my gun, of course; but you were actually right. By Halloween, I couldn't think of anything else but those dead eyes and the blood. I still see it when I close my own eyes; I can't get it out of my dreams."

"I was worried about that."

"I know," she frowned. "I needed some mothering and caught the first flight I could get here. The healing power of chicken pot pie and knitted comforters, I guess."

"Has it worked?"

"Not really. Maybe a little."

"We found your gun," I said softly. "We're testing it now."

Sylvia snapped her head at me. "You *what*? What right--"

"The water bottles," Vasily cut her off. "The ones in the back of his truck? They're yours."

"Of course they are!" she said curtly. "He needed to move something - I forget what it was now - and thought the bottles could stabilize whatever it was he was moving."

"I'm sorry," I said. "Are you actually telling me that he asked to borrow nine five-gallon jugs of water - some empty, some full - to move something?"

"Yes," she said defensively. "I drove his truck down to my place and loaded it up for him."

"When?"

"Last week."

"Before he spoke with Doctor Kellerman?"

"Yes - just after."

"Three on either side, three across the top?" Vasily asked.

"Yeah," she said, slightly unsure of herself. "Now that I think about it, he'd given me some pretty specific but pretty weird instructions."

"And you didn't think it odd that he didn't ask you to help move the actual item?"

Sylvia looked up at us again and took another deep drag on her cigarette. "Ingmar was a wonderful gentleman, Chief," she said as she exhaled another cloud. I tried not to cough. "A bit loopy as any scientist, perhaps; more so the further his cancer progressed. It didn't seem all that odd at the time."

"Can you describe your movements from Saturday at eight in the morning, to Monday at the same time?"

Sylvia frowned. "I saw Ingmar during my run Saturday morning; I picked up the gun from him about eight-thirty. I left for the Colonial a bit after nine and worked the Symposium until the wee hours of the morning. I stayed over at the hotel - I have a room for when things get nutty - and got home after nine on Sunday evening after a lousy day of making scientists happy." She crushed her cigarette out inside the cup she'd used for her coffee. "You know where I was on Monday morning."

"And the Colonial will be able to verify that?"

"I imagine."

"Do you have a smart doorbell?" Vasily asked.

Sylvia looked surprised. "I do; I put it in a few months ago. Most of us on that street have one."

"Even Pelletier?" I asked.

"Are you kidding?" she laughed. "He's not exactly well versed in modern technology."

"Will you allow us to review the footage on your doorbell?"

"If it will get me out of the doghouse, yes, Chief. It'll definitely confirm my goings-and-comings. If you have paper, I'll give you my password right now."

Vasily flipped to blank page in his notebook and slid it to her.

"How long are you planning on staying here in Florida?" I asked as she scribbled something on the paper.

"A few more days. My return flight isn't until the sixteenth."

"So, you were planning on going home?"

"Yes," she said, looking up at me. "I have no reason not to."

"Good," I said.

"How much trouble am I in, Chief?"

I tried to smile gently as I stood. "I'm not sure," I replied honestly. "I'll let you know when I am."

"That's not very comforting," she frowned.

"Welcome to my world, Sylvia."

Thirty-Three

"Do you believe her?"

We were sitting in a Denny's close to the police station grabbing breakfast for a late lunch. Vasily and I had some time to kill before we needed to get back to the airport and we'd been running on the overpriced peanuts we'd been given - despite paying through the nose for our last-minute airfare. "Well," I said as I poured myself more coffee from the carafe the waitress had left behind. "We now have four perfectly reasonable explanations for our various suspects movements for the weekend, along with similarly reasonable explanations for why they had access to or were in possession of a Glock. Sylvia, perhaps, has the most heart-rending reason of all, but like the others, I can't disprove it until the Crime Lab gets back to us."

"So, you think she was acting compassionately, then? And *only* compassionately?"

I sipped my coffee. "The water bottles still bug me, and I can't exactly explain why."

Vasily scooped up some of his massive omelet and chewed thoughtfully. "It was such an odd request from Pelletier. And she didn't seem willing to question it." He spread some orange marmalade on his wheat toast. "And what do you suppose would have fit inside the space? I'm having a hard time seeing any sort of furniture or other item that would comfortably nestle within those bottles."

"I don't think he was moving anything, if that's what you're asking," I said. My half-eaten chocolate-chip pancakes lay in front of me, unappetizing for some reason. "What if... what if no one was supposed to have shot him?" I pondered. "I've long thought this was planned, but maybe we're looking at the wrong person who planned it."

Vasily looked at me. "The angle's wrong for suicide."

"For the shot that we know about? Sure. But let's suppose for a moment that Ingmar is totally despondent, knowing he's not going to get his drugs. He knows he must sell the house to pay off the bills; maybe he confides in the wrong people about his plans. I don't know that part yet. But I'm reasonably confident saying when he had Sylvia bring him those water bottles, he'd intended on pulling the trigger himself."

"I still don't see how they fit into his plan."

"Simple," I said. "We know he was shot sitting up - the bullet angle tells us that. But if he had done it himself, I'd wager he would have realized a suicide would be messy - messy enough that his real estate agent would have had trouble selling the house. All that blood everywhere tends to drive the price down."

"As it has," Vasily nodded. "The sleeping pills would have been easier."

"Exactly. So he creates a little nest in the bed of his truck - he's thought this through, like a true scientist, and knows that the truck can be towed away and will contain all of that messiness in one easy-to-move package."

Vasily nodded deeper. "But the bottles?"

"Two reasons, I think. Whenever he'd originally intended to do it, he assumed it would be a typical late Fall day and likely to be cold. The ambient temperature in the bed of the truck would have stayed warm enough to keep everything fluid and his body moveable. Remember, he would have wanted to be discovered fairly quickly - the murder, though planned, just happened to take place with the same parameters in play."

"And the second?"

"They would have held the bullet," I said simply. "Or slowed it down significantly. He thought this through enough, I believe, that he would have leaned up against the full bottles in the rear to keep the bullet from going too far and significantly damaging the house or the truck. The murderer didn't realize that."

"Hence the angle of the bullet we found."

"Exactly. That's the part that makes it murder and not suicide. And yet, out of everyone we've talked to, I still don't have a compelling motive among *any* of them. Maybe, *maybe* one of them. But nothing that I could go to the DA with at this point."

"Not Sylvia?"

I looked at the congealing syrup on my plate. "I don't think so." I paused. "Damn it. Maybe." My eyes came up to Vasily's. "I hate this case."

"I don't blame you," he laughed.

I only half heard him; I had my coffee mug in my hands and was watching a stray grind as it circled the interior. "Sylvia said he was trying to get end-of-life drugs," I murmured.

"Yes," Vasily responded.

I looked up. "Did you finish the financials on Ingmar?"

"Mostly."

"He was selling his house, you said. If Elaine sold it short, it wouldn't cover all of the outstanding mortgages on it, right?"

"No," he said, turning to his backpack and pulling out his tablet. Scrolling for a moment, his eyes hit something, and he read it. "The most optimistic scenario left him short about three-hundred thousand."

There comes a point in every case when the mist finally clears and the through line from the beginning to the end becomes evident. I swirled my mug, partial smile on my lips as I watched the coffee grind move. "His life insurance was worth half a million, wasn't it?" I asked, looking up.

Vasily raised an eyebrow and then returned to his iPad. "Five-hundred-fifty, actually," he said as his eyes came back to mine. "How did you know?"

"Is the University the beneficiary?"

"Yes," he said.

"How much do you want to bet that Sylvia wasn't the only one aware that Ingmar wanted to check out early?" I asked, setting aside the coffee.

Vasily started to smile. "You'll never get her to admit to it."

"Oh, I think I will," I said. "I imagine when you check with the insurance company that issued the policy, they'll tell you it has an exclusion for suicide. Most do."

"Shit," he said. "That changes things."

"Does it ever," I said as I flagged down the waitress for the check. "Let's get out of here; we have a plane to catch."

Thirty-Four

Our connection in Atlanta was delayed, resulting in our returning to the Portland International Jetport close to midnight. The subsequent drive to Windeport, though expedited by a slightly illegal use of lights, still put us back in the apartment at two in the morning. The power appeared to have been restored, and a note on the breakfast counter told us that Suzanne had returned to Charlie's farmhouse. Part of me was a bit sad to see the note.

I stripped off everything and fell into bed, but sleep refused to come despite my (unusually) eschewing of any coffee on the drive back from Portland. I felt like I finally had my hands around the case and knew what we were likely going to find on those Ring doorbells along Ocean View Avenue. I hoped we'd only need Sylvia's footage, but if we had more from neighbors, it would seal the deal.

Tossing and turning, I finally got up at five and tossed on my running tights and a thermal top. I didn't have the patience to go to swim practice; as I laced my running shoes and pulled on my knit cap, I knew a run through town would allow me to make an unannounced visit to the scene of the crime while burning off my anxiety.

I tip-toed past Vasily's room and then hopped down the steps two at a time. Once outside, I turned on my headlamp and slid into my gloves, then started down the side street to Route One at an easy pace. I'd long entertained the notion of entering a triathlon at some point but had only mastered the running and swimming parts of the discipline.

I didn't run very often - usually only when it was part of our dryland exercise routine at practice - but over the years had come to appreciate the clarity of mind that could appear two- or three-miles in.

The snow crunched beneath my sneakers, and I kept watch out for patches of ice. The second round of snow had come and gone as promised, and Public Works had scraped most of the sidewalks down to bare concrete, so there was little to worry about. Still, it wouldn't do for the police chief to twist an ankle or break a leg.

Main Street was quiet, lit by the streetlights along either side. I could see some of the town holiday decorations had already started to appear, including the ribbon of greenery that stretched across Route One in front of the Public Safety building -- a bit too early for my tastes, really. As I ran beneath it, I realized I didn't yet know where I was going to be spending the holiday myself. It was a good bet that Charlie would not be exactly welcoming after what I'd put her through.

Turning onto Aspen Street, the sidewalk narrowed a bit for the older neighborhood. The streetlights faded after a block, leaving my headlamp as the primary way to illuminate my path forward. I noted for the first time the round, illuminated signature of those smart doorbells; it seemed the closer I got to the waterfront, the more I saw of them.

Ocean View appeared and I crossed the street once more after waiting for a late-model Buick to pass. Many of the houses here were dark, but a few had a light here or there indicating they were occupied. My parents had long wanted to live down in this area of town, long considered the most desirable section of the village. I wondered if Ingmar had realized that, or simply enjoyed his proximity to the ocean.

I rounded a slight curve in the road as it followed the shoreline and realized for the first time that through a quirk of alignment, Sylvia's bungalow faced Ingmar's, though it was still several houses apart. As I got closer, I noted her Ring doorbell and saw it not only covered her driveway, but also his as well.

Interesting.

A moment later, I pulled up at the end of his driveway and paused my exercise timer. Slowly I moved up into the carport, noting the driveway had been shoveled. I presumed that meant Elaine was still working the sale as best as she could. Standing about where the truck had been parked, I turned a complete circle, letting my headlamp catch the hidden depths of the area before stopping facing Sylvia's home.

It was further away than I'd thought it would be, making me worry the doorbell might not have the video I wanted, but then again, it might. It was a card I was willing to play.

Now that the truck was gone, I could also see how visible the driveway and carport were from the street. Ocean View wasn't a thoroughfare, to be sure, but it was one of a handful of streets that provided right-of-way access to the beach. Villagers or people randomly driving through town were attracted to the rugged shore in the summer months, and sometimes even in late Fall, so Ingmar would have had a reasonable expectation someone would have found him had he gone through with his plan. Just not apparently this past Sunday.

Fate appeared to have a cruel streak.

I snapped my timer back on and headed back toward Main Street; I made good time on the three-mile loop and was just back at the apartment a bit before six. Vasily's car was gone, so I knew he'd gone to practice, and I'd see him at the station later. Pausing at the door to the stairwell, though, I stared thoughtfully at the tire tracks he'd left behind. He'd been nothing but professional since that unguarded moment in Boston, and for the first time I wondered how hard it was for him to keep his feelings in check. That was followed by no small amount of guilt that I was incapable of being more than his friend; it was an unsustainable cycle that would end badly at some point. That thought tore me up inside, but I had no idea how to make it better for him -- for both of us.

The hot water from my shower felt good after the pleasant chill of the run; I made a smoothie and chased it with my first cup of coffee for the day before heading to the station. I was early enough that Beverly was still at the Reception/Intake desk; she nodded to me as I passed, engrossed in a call from a concerned citizen regarding a missing cat. It was not an unusual call for us, and for some reason, missing pets always seemed to tug at my heartstrings the most. I had even been known to scour the county to locate a missing feline or canine myself.

Hanging my jacket up on the door, I wandered to the Keurig and made my second cup of coffee, then headed for the window behind my desk to stare at the fields as the sun slowly began to work its way into the sky. It was still heavily overcast, so essentially the day was upgrading from solid gray to something a bit lighter.

"Chief?"

I turned as Vasily moved to my desk. "Internet is back," he said as he sat in the left guest chair, his customary choice. "But this came by courier from the Crime Lab just now," he added, handing me a manilla envelope.

I took it and noted the seal was broken with an arched eyebrow.

"Sorry boss," he smiled wickedly. "I had to know."

"Indeed," I laughed as I pulled open the flap and slid out the mass of paperwork. Quickly, I scanned the precis on the cover sheet and slowly started to nod. "There it is," I said as I slid it back into the envelope.

"Yes," he smiled wider. "I'll drive."

"Good," I said, "for I just poured this cup of coffee."

Thirty-Five

Vasily parked the SUV in the red zone at the front of the College of Agriculture just as class change appeared to be taking place. Students were quite literally everywhere, making it nearly impossible to navigate a clear pathway to the front of the building. Somehow, we managed to part the waters and get in; the clearly visible guns at our waists may have helped in some small way.

Barbara Thompson was in her usual customary place when we pushed through the door into the business office and looked up over her glasses at our entry. "Chief," she smiled. "Are you here to arrest her? *Please* tell me you're here to arrest her. It'll make my week."

"That's an odd thing to ask," I said, somewhat startled at her reaction.

She shrugged. "I gave you enough access to our financials to put Doctor Bedard behind bars for life." She snorted. "Well, what little she has left, I wager."

"Indeed," I smiled. "Is she in?"

"Yes." She pointed to the corner suite. "Right that way, gentlemen."

I nodded as we passed her desk, and asked Vasily quietly, "Is she right?"

"About the finances?" He shrugged. "Maybe. I'm not a forensic accountant, but even I could tell some odd shenanigans have gone on here."

"One more thing to tell the District Attorney," I said as I knocked on the faux wood grained door. Bedard's name had been stenciled onto it in rather gaudy gold script.

"Come in," she rasped in her smoker's voice.

The door swung inward, and we entered the massive office as apparently befitted the Dean of the College. A massive CEO-style desk was angled in the corner, with two couches in the other arrayed around a low coffee table. On the wall opposite the windows, a small bookcase had been hung in the space above a countertop sporting the usual bar items; I wondered if she used the gin and whiskey to seal the deal with donors, or if it was more for her own use.

"Doctor Bedard," I said as we took up positions behind the two comfortable looking guest chairs facing the massive desk. "I have a few follow-up questions for you."

"Not really the time, Chief," she said as she ruffled paper on her desk and avoided eye contact. The heavy odor of smoke hovered in the room, and my eyes fell upon a lit cigarette perched upon the edge of an ashtray made in the shape of the State of Maine.

"I believe campus is tobacco-free these days," I observed.

"So, arrest me," she said as she pulled a file out and opened it.

I let that pass. "When did you find out about the life insurance policy?" I asked.

Bedard tensed and stopped reading the contents of the folder. Her eyes came up and met mine as she reached for the cigarette and took a deep pull against it. "What policy?" she countered as she blew a cloud out and away from us.

"We know that Ingmar had depleted what reserves he had to fund Menard's research," I said.

"The grants had run out," she said.

"Is that what he told you?"

"Yes," she said. "And he said there wasn't anything to do about it." She sucked another long breath from the cigarette and leaned back into her chair. "I thought he was lying to me, to be honest. Once he'd discovered the... issues... we were having with the research, I was convinced that he'd started to redirect funding elsewhere."

"But he wasn't," Vasily said.

"No," she nodded slowly. "I had Barbara pull the financials for me and saw that we really were out of money."

"You couldn't turn to your donors? Or those companies that you were wining and dining at the Symposium?"

"No," she repeated. "Even the one I met with last week had gone into a wait-and-see stance. Not one of them was willing to invest in us without solid results." She stabbed what was left of her cigarette into the ashtray and lit another from the pack on the desk. "Like I told you earlier, he'd managed to get the word out to all of our potential investors that our little super potato was anything but." Waving the match she'd used to put out the flame, she took a long drag before dramatically blowing out another cloud to emphasize her exasperation. "Damn him."

"When did you learn about the life insurance?" I asked again.

She looked at me over the cigarette in her mouth, a wisp of smoke trailing upward as she spoke. "Five years ago," she said. "He'd announced it at a faculty meeting. He was so damn proud that his final act as a human would be to fund our department."

"That money would have come in handy, then, given your cash crunch."

Bedard snorted. "We weren't gonna see any of it until he died," she said unemotionally.

"You knew he had cancer," I said simply. "So that sped up the timeline."

She looked at me, and I knew I'd played the right hunch. "Yes," she said. "He was terminal. And I'll be frank: it was just desserts that he found out so soon after he'd screwed us over with his actions on the research."

"Did he speak openly about wanting to end his own life?"

"Not initially," she said. "But we all knew he was in pain, and there were whispers among the staff that he'd been trying to get his doctor to sign off on something." Her anger flamed a bit. "If he had, it would've cancelled his policy, damn him. So even in the end, he was looking for a way to screw us over again."

"So, you... *encouraged* him not to," I said. "Down in the tunnel."

Bedard looked at me and smiled slightly. "Yes," she confirmed.

"How'd you get him down there?"

She smiled wider. "We'd been an item, the two of us," she said. "It wasn't hard to fake him out with just enough tenderness; in the end, he understood my position and agreed to not end his life that way."

"In fact, your little threat spurred him to seek other methods," Vasily said.

"Really," she frowned. "I guess I don't have the same effect on men I once did."

"Certainly not men dying from terminal cancer," I allowed. "But you knew *that*, too."

"What do you mean?" she asked, her eyes flashing.

"It was your gun that killed him," I said simply. "And your prints were the only other ones at his house."

"So what?" she asked. "Maybe I loaned it to him. He did ask for one. I'm sure I couldn't have been the only one, either."

"I'm sure he did, just like I am sure you would never have given it to him. Like you said, suicide didn't benefit the University. Or you."

"Exactly."

"But murder would. The policy pays in full."

She looked at me. "He pulled the trigger," she said. "It wasn't me."

"Maybe," I said. "I'm going to wait on that until I see the video."

"The *what*?"

"I was rather surprised myself," I said. "But it seems a number of houses here in Windeport have those smart doorbells; as it turns out, there's one pointing right at Ingmar's carport." I paused.

Bedard had gone still and was watching me intently.

"I am fairly sure I'm going to see you pull up to his house on Sunday. Maybe you rang his doorbell, maybe you knocked; somehow, you got him to agree to speak to you one more time. I don't know how you convinced him, but ultimately he wound up in the bed of that truck, your gun in his mouth." I paused again. "But *you* were holding the gun."

Stony faced, she took an even longer drag on the cigarette.

"Then he changes his mind. He sits up, deciding perhaps that the drugs from Doctor Kellerman would be easier to use." I caught the flicker on Bedard's face. "You didn't know?" I asked, looking at Vasily. "She'd agreed to get him the prescription."

"I didn't. He never mentioned it."

"Regardless," I continued. "You were done waiting. He was ill, and weak, and likely couldn't put up much of a fight; I think you snapped and pulled the trigger, going through with your own plan for a significant influx of cash for the University.

"All you needed to do was get the bullet and the shell casing and you'd be clear; the street was deserted with most of the homeowners already in Florida. Except Ingmar wasn't arranged the way he needed to be; the shell took longer to find than you planned on, and as a result you had to return to the Colonial in order to be seen where you needed to be at the right time."

"You left the bullet, and we found it before you could return yourself," Vasily finished.

"It was a reasonably good plan," I said, "save for two shortcomings."

"Really," she snorted. "And what would those be, hypothetically?"

"One: you left the bullet behind."

She rolled her eyes as she stabbed out the cigarette and lit her third. "And the second?"

"Pelletier was your mystery donor," I said. "His house has a double mortgage, and the estate will be using the life insurance to pay off the shortfall from the sale of the bungalow. It won't leave more than a few thousand dollars to the University when all is said and done."

"Say what?" she asked pointedly. "He *what?*"

"The magical funding? It came out of his own pocket."

"No shit," she said, eyes widening. "Now I understand why he was so upset about the research results."

"He was your first investor," I nodded. "He believed in it up until he saw the raw data."

"Damn." She looked away and out the windows. "What now, then?" she asked.

"I'll need you to come with us, please," I said. "You have two choices at this point. Tell us everything and I seek what might pass for leniency from our DA. Or you get a lawyer and fight us." I leaned on her desk. "But I will win if you do. So, you might want to keep that in mind."

"He was dying anyway," she said, still looking out the window.

"Ingmar Pelletier had the right to go out however he wanted." I looked to Vasily. "You took that away from him. No one gets the ability to do that, Doctor."

Bedard looked up at me finally, resignation in her eyes. "Let me cancel my appointments for the rest of the day," she said as she reached for her desk phone.

"You might want to go a bit further than that," I said. "A *lot* further."

Thirty-Six

"*Cataclysm!*" I cried from my crouch next to the bed. The young cancer patient's eyes went wide as I released the wad of tissues I'd kept hidden in the palm of my costumed hand; I'd carefully colored them grey to look like ash. "You... you did it, Chat!" she said with awe; she was so weak, her voice was barely a whisper.

"With your help, Milady," I said as I revealed the purple butterfly I'd been hiding behind my back. "Are you ready?"

She nodded, her ladybug-themed head wrap catching the light. Carefully, she tapped the butterfly with a finger, saying as loud as she could: "Miraculous Ladybug!"

My masked eyes crinkled as I smiled - it wasn't exactly right, per se, but close enough for me. "Good work! Hawkmoth has gone down in flames again."

Despite her sunken expression, the smile that appeared on her face lit her features with warmth. I leaned down and gently kissed her on the forehead. "Meow I need to go see if there are any other akumas on this floor," I whispered into her ear. "Purromise me you'll be on the lookout?"

"I will, Chat!" she smiled as she leaned back into her pillow. The nurse standing on the other side moved in to readjust her IV as I stood. "Bye!"

"Goodbye!" I waved as I dropped to all fours and did my best to lope out on hands and feet. It looked far easier than it was.

Suzanne was coming out of the room beside mine, attired once more in her Ladybug costume. "I'll let Chat know," she was saying to her new friend. "But honestly, it'll just go to his head."

I found myself smiling; as a newly-minted physician with privileges at Maine Medical Center, she'd quickly heard that a nurse in the Barbara Bush Children's Wing had put out the call for superheroes to swing through on Thanksgiving to help brighten up the day for kids who were stuck there during the holiday. Knowing that we both still had our costumes from Halloween, it didn't take much for her to convince me to help, and joined by Vasily, the three of us had driven down the night before so we could be in the hospital first thing in the morning.

It helped that Charlie had banned me from the farm through the new year, leaving me with no place to be myself; besides, Vasily had unexpectedly decided to go visit his family for a week, so it would have been a fairly lonely day had Suzanne not rescued me. That made me start, and I pulled out my faux baton; Vasily had managed to adjust it such that my iPhone fit snugly into the center of it if I popped it open, which I did to check the time. He had a one o'clock flight, and we'd need to leave soon to get him to the airport for his departure.

As I closed the baton and replaced it at the small of my back, Suzanne caught my eye and wandered toward me. "Hey kitty," she smiled, a megawatt affair that I had grown to love. Despite my having nearly arrested her, she seemed quite happy to be in my company. We'd more or less become a couple since Bedard had plead guilty to murder and had headed off to the Thomaston State Prison. "Do we have to go already? I'm just getting warmed up."

I smiled at that. "We've been here four hours already, Milady," I said, staying in character. "But yes, we should go soon."

She tapped my bell with a gloved hand. "All right. One more room?"

"Sure," I said, laughing. "Anything for you, bugaboo."

There was a snorted chuckle from the nurse's station behind us, and we both turned to see a middle-aged woman in vibrant red scrubs and silver hair trying hard not to laugh. "You two are *perfect*," she said.

"Don't you mean *purrfect*?" I asked.

"Of course," she chuckled. "You even have me believing you're really in love," she said, clasping her hands together.

"Maybe we are," Suzanne said, her blue eyes twinkling behind the Ladybug mask.

"Maybe," I said, winking at her.

"Thank you for doing this for us. It means the world to the kids."

"Our pleasure," I said. "We have to drop our colleague off at the airport, but we'll come right back if you'll have us."

"Are you kidding?" the nurse laughed. "The kids would love it. We'll save you what passes for turkey from the cafeteria if you like."

"Deal."

Suzanne and I visited with one more young boy who was suffering from the later stages of cystic fibrosis before finding Vasily waiting for us at the nurse's station. I was a little surprised to see he'd already donned his civilian clothes. "What?" I teased good naturedly. "Not going to California as Thor?"

He rolled his eyes. "I have enough issues with my father; showing up in that outfit would set the wrong tone for the visit."

"I can imagine. Let me change--"

"Actually, Sean, I'm just going to take an Uber."

"Oh, save your money," I said good naturedly. "Suze and I can get you there in a jiffy."

"No," he said firmly. "It would only make this harder."

Something in his expression caught me. "Harder?" I asked. "Dude, it's just a few miles to the airport from here. I know my way around Portland."

"It's not that. Look, can I talk to you for a moment?" he asked, before looking over to Suzanne. "Uh, if you don't mind, Doctor...?"

Sensing something herself, Suzanne nodded. "Certainly. Let me know when you're ready," she added as she moved to another room in the wing.

I turned back to Vasily, hard enough that the bell at my collar sang our happily. "I feel like I am missing something here."

"You are," he said as he gently grabbed my costumed bicep and moved us into a quiet portion of the waiting room a few paces from the nurse's station.

"So... this is kind of awkward."

"Okay," I said, crossing my arms as I leaned back against the wall.

"I'm not coming back."

I blinked my masked eyes. "Here? To Maine?"

"To Windeport," he said.

From down the hallway, I heard Suzanne crying out, "*Miraculous Ladybug!*" It seemed to accentuate the odd situation.

Staring at my best friend, I tried to process what he'd just said. "How long?" I asked quietly.

"For a while," he nodded and looked away. "I... I think it's for the best. For both of us."

I swallowed. "You *hate* California," I pointed out.

"I do," he said. "But I've accepted a position in a small city south of Los Angeles. I'll make it work. Lord knows it will be a more accepting environment than here," he added.

I was uncertain if he meant Windeport in general... or me in particular. "Vasily," I said, "I don't know what to say. You're my right-hand; I thought you loved the work. Loved the town."

"It's not the *job*, damn it," he said tightly. "It's you. It's *always* been you. I don't want to be your right hand. I want *you*." His eyes flashed with that same desire I'd seen in Boston. "And it means I can't work for you any longer. Or be near you."

"So... you're leaving? Just like that?" I felt like someone was hammering me in the stomach.

"Yes," he said.

My gut was twisting inside out. There had rarely been a day in the last fifteen years that the two of us hadn't been together. The thought of not seeing him, perhaps for a significant period, sent shockwaves through me. "Why do I have a feeling that you're not going to want to keep in touch?"

He smiled as he brushed back his blond hair. "That is why you're the chief, Chief, and I'm just a lowly detective." Vasily leaned close and kissed me on the cheek, softly. "Maybe, when I'm ready, I'll reach out. But until then, this is the way it has to be."

A turmoil of emotions simmered as I observed: "This feels more like a breakup of a bad relationship than a goodbye."

"You're not far off," he nodded sadly. Picking up his duffel bag, he smiled again. "Goodbye, Sean. I wish you well."

"Vasily--"

"Don't," he said, and I could see tears were forming in his eyes. "This really is for the best."

I blinked and nodded, realizing that my own eyes appeared to be watering up. "All right then. But no goodbyes," I said, quoting something I'd once heard at a funeral. "Just good memories."

He nodded again, turned, and walked deliberately down the hallway to the corner; he rounded it without looking back once and then was gone from the ward.

And my life.

I stood there, leaning against the wall in my Chat costume, and dropped my chin to my chest as the tears started to roll. Suzanne appeared and placed a gloved hand to my bicep. "Sean? What's wrong? Where's Vasily?"

I pulled Suzanne into my chest and buried my head in her hair. "Gone," was all I could get out before I sank to the floor with her in my arms and started to weep at the full measure of what I'd lost.

Thirty-Seven

Epilogue

It took longer than normal to close escrow on my new home, but in the end, between the fire sale price and ten years of rent payments to my father, my new mortgage made barely a dent in my finances. Two weeks before Christmas, I was sitting on the bare floor of the living room in what had been Ingmar Pelletier's home, and watched the grey waves of the ocean as they broke over the shoals guarding Windeport Harbor.

The sea reflected my bleak mood; moving out of the old pharmacy building had felt like the closing of a chapter in my life I'd not really wanted to leave behind. Suzanne had been an immense help, both in physically carting my stuff between the old and new spaces, but also emotionally. Packing and then moving had seemed like a one-two punch that had started with Vasily's abrupt departure for California.

I'd felt his loss keenly. His old position was posted now, of course, but I had no great desire to try and replace him, perhaps on the outside chance that he'd change his mind and return. But that was unlikely; his new department had already made the call to have his packet sent over, making his new posting final.

There was a clatter in the kitchen behind me, and I turned to see an embarrassed Suzanne picking up what was left of a coffee mug from the linoleum. "I'm sorry," she said.

I stood up and went to help, picking my way through the boxes she'd been helping me unpack. "No worries," I smiled. "That was an ugly mug anyway."

"Maybe we can glue it back together," she suggested.

Looking at the piece in my hand, I turned the shard around and watched as it caught the light. "Not everything can be patched back up," I said in a burst of insight. "Sometimes, you sweep aside the pieces and then replace what was broken with something new."

I looked into Suzanne's deep blue eyes. "Something better."

Suzanne looked at me quizzically. "Are you okay?"

"Yes," I said, returning her smile, suddenly feeling better than I had in weeks.

Acknowledgement

Despite what you may have heard, writing isn't a solo profession. Oh, sure, you can start off that way, sitting in front of your word processor and immersing yourself in the universe you are creating. That's a good thing, of course, because unless you are fully committed to the people and places you are crafting, your readers won't be, either. But there is a fine line between what you have written and what you *think* you've written, and that is when writing becomes something closer to a shared experience. No writer should be without a trusted group of beta readers, people who will give you the pure, unvarnished truth about what you have created.

It's one of the most nerve-wracking experiences I've ever gone though, but also one of the most fulfilling. As I write this, I've penned three novels in this series, and as I embark on the fourth, I know for sure the wise observations, suggestions and, yes, even corrections have made my stories even better. I cannot say *thank you* enough to these amazing people:

Charlotte, Tristan and Lisa, aka the Writing (S)quad of Doom: thank you for keeping me honest, consistent, and realistic. I can't tell you how nice it is to randomly throw out questions about *anything* and getting amazing help in return. (Sadly, though, I couldn't bear to take the either the coffee or fruit references out.)

Brett: getting your thumbs up on my earliest draft kept me going through all the successive edits. Thank you, my friend, for being willing to dive in.

Kristin: a fresh set of eyes helped immensely to round out some of the backstories that appear in the final version. I can't wait to share the next novels with you!

Dad: given you love this genre as much as I do, I was scared to death to have you review the manuscript. Your stamp of approval means more to me than you can ever know.

And finally, my wife, **Paula**: your quiet support kept me grounded as I worked through the challenges of this story. You are my muse and my biggest fan, and there is absolutely no way I could have done this without you. My love is yours, always and forever.

--C

October 24, 2020

About the Author

Born and raised in Maine, Chris has spent nearly three decades as an IT nerd, writing just about everything *other* than a novel in the process. That changed in early 2019 when he was advised to find a way to wind down from his day job; sifting through his options, he recalled a childhood ambition to become a writer and quickly found himself weaving an entirely new world from the comfort of his laptop. *Blindsided* is his first book, part of a planned series featuring both Chief Sean Colbeth and Detective Vasily Korsokovach.

Despite his love for the Northeast, the author escaped the cold for Arizona, where he currently resides with his beautiful wife, two cats, and a Shar-Pei mix that insists on being walked regularly.

Lightning Source UK Ltd.
Milton Keynes UK
UKHW021858070121
376641UK00009B/577/J